Ghosts and Pink Candles

A Witch's Cove Mystery
Book 14

Vella Day

Birthdays should be happy. Mine was until a magical ring caused me to see many, many ghosts.

It was a present from my mom. She'd found the ring tucked away in a closet that her mom had asked to pass down to me. The stone was a match to my pink pendant. Dare I hope it was magical, too? Turns out it was, because when I tried it on, I saw them—them being about ten ghosts floating around in my aunt's restaurant. Oh, my.

Naturally, I couldn't wait to find out what was going on. It wasn't that I hadn't seen ghosts before, just not so many at one time. Note: I took off the ring right away. Even I was a little scared.

Eventually a friend of my Nana's appeared to ask if I could find a missing friend of hers. Sure, no problem. It's what I did, being an amateur sleuth, and all. Armed with her name, I set out to pick the brains of the gossip queens, but what I found out made seeing ghosts a piece of cake.

Thankfully my wonderful boyfriend and my talking pick iguana familiar will help me figure it out. Stop on by the Tiki Hut Grill to get the latest update on this very bizarre case.

Chapter One

"HAPPY BIRTHDAY TO you. Happy birthday to you. Happy birthday, dear Glinda, happy birthday to you. How o-old are you?"

My ears rang from the off-key voices—two of which belonged to my parents. Both were tone deaf, which made birthdays a little painful. However, now that the song was over, I could focus on the good stuff.

In front of me was a huge two-layer chocolate cake with chocolate and pink frosting. My aunt had made it—pastries were her specialty—and she'd rimmed the bottom layer with cherries, because she knew I loved them. The sprinkles were a nice added touch, too.

Almost everyone my aunt and mother had invited to this party had shown up, and I hoped there would be enough dessert for the twenty-plus people at The Tiki Hut Grill. Knowing my efficient Aunt Fern, she had another cake in the back just in case.

"Blow out the candles, sweetie," my mother urged.

Even though I was now twenty-eight, there were only five candles on top—pink of course—which was fine by me. Because there was something rather unsanitary about having breath pour over a cake, I wet my fingers and doused the flames quickly. I might be a witch, but I didn't have the power to extinguish the flames with a wave of a hand or by tossing out a quick spell. That talent belonged to someone else.

The rather sweet sulfur scent that I pleasantly associated with séances and Christmas teased my nostrils. I might be the only one, but I liked the smell.

"Did you make a wish?" my mother asked.

No. In truth, I didn't believe that birthday wishes came true, so why make them? My mom, however, was a true believer. She also was a true believer in the *Wizard of Oz*, so you be the judge about her. "Sure, but I'm not telling you what I wished for."

She grinned. "Whatever it is, I hope it comes true."

"Me, too." It might if I'd made one.

"Are you going to cut the cake, open the presents, or just stare at everything?" My boyfriend, Jaxson Harrison, fully understood that I was prone to daydreaming.

He was the love of my life, despite our relationship not starting out under the best of circumstances. After a rather tumultuous beginning, we learned to appreciate each other's talents. Turns out, Jaxson was the ying to my yang. Who knew? As a result of how well we complemented each other, we started The Pink Iguana Sleuth agency a year ago. I like to think we've helped a lot of people in that time.

"I'm just admiring Aunt Fern's handiwork." I turned to my aunt. "Why don't you cut the cake? You know I'd just make a mess."

She and my mom didn't have to nod with such force—and my mother's eye roll was totally unnecessary—but I wasn't offended in the least. I could take orders and serve food, but preparing a meal or baking a cake wasn't my forte.

"Sure, dear," my aunt said.

"And, Mom, can you pass the plates around?"

"Of course."

In quick order, my aunt cut the cake into perfectly even pieces, something I never could have achieved. As my mom gave out the dessert to the guests, I checked the assortment of friends who were there. They ranged from the sheriff and his deputy, along with both of their girlfriends, to the many gossip queens in town—which included my Aunt Fern. Naturally, my cousin, Rihanna was there with her boyfriend, Gavin, who was the medical examiner's son. Considering Witch's Cove was a small town, it didn't surprise me that everyone seemed to be connected to someone else either by blood or by job.

My aunt had cordoned off the back patio of her restaurant, including the Tiki Hut bar itself, for our party. This venue was spectacular in large part because the restaurant sat on an expansive white beach on the Gulf of Mexico. The festivities were being held after sunset, which meant the lights from the nearby boats, set against the backdrop of the Florida summer sky, twinkled in the distance. The warm, slightly salty scented breeze wafted off the water, creating a relaxing and calm environment.

Since no one was mopping sweat off their foreheads, the guests seemed to be comfortable on the outdoor patio. And yes, I had asked Aunt Fern to put several bottles of bug spray out, just in case.

Should the partygoers choose to imbibe, drinks were free tonight.

Once we had our cake in hand, we all took a seat at the long table that could easily handle twenty-five people. Only after everyone finished eating did I plan to open the presents. It didn't seem to matter that I asked people not to buy me anything. They all did. From the shape and size of the gifts, a few appeared to be bottles of wine, which I was happy to have.

I sat next to Jaxson, of course. My talking pink iguana familiar, Iggy, decided not to come. He understood a few of my friends might be a bit squeamish when it came to seeing an animal at the table. Iggy didn't see himself as anything other than human, but my nine-pound wonder was not one of us, despite his ability to communicate.

My mom and dad, who ran the funeral home next door, sat across from me. Since they always seemed to be busy, it was really nice to be with them for an evening.

Next to my mom was Penny Carsted, my friend who I had waitressed with for over three years. She was with her beau, Hunter Ashwell, who happened to be the forest ranger, as well as one of our resident werewolves—though few in town knew that about him.

"How's the landlord business going?" my mom asked, jarring me out of my reverie.

"No problems so far, though remember, we just signed the papers a few weeks ago."

When the owner of the building across the street decided he wanted nothing more to do with the issues of this town, he put the strip of stores up for sale. Since Jaxson and I had been paid extremely well for our most bizarre case—long story—we decided (okay, I had suggested) that we buy the entire strip of stores on the main street. I feared an unknown landlord might come in and impose high rents on these hard working people. Not only that, being the owner would guarantee us a monthly income.

"Have you rented the yarn shop space yet?" my mom asked.

The first owner left due to family issues, and the next owner was murdered. I hoped the new owner would have better luck. "Not yet."

"I'm hoping a computer store will want to rent the space." Jaxson held up a hand. "And in case either of you hear of someone with technological abilities interested in a storefront, please send him our way."

My mom smiled. She understood Jaxson's penchant for all things that had to do with computers. "Will do."

Jaxson was amazing with technology-based items. He could find almost any snippet of information we needed on a person—within legal limits, of course. Without his help, our business might not have succeeded.

"Glinda, what would you like to see occupy that space?" my mom asked.

That was easy. "You know I love books, but I understand that bookstores aren't very profitable. Honestly, I just want a good owner." Way to skirt the issue, right? And by a good owner, I meant one who paid attention to things—which many people would call a gossip. Hey, what could I say? It's the gas to our sleuthing engine.

"Good luck, dear."

We chatted about the funeral business—never a real cheery or appropriate topic for a party—so when I noticed people had finished their dessert, I nodded to Jaxson. It was his cue to tell me to open the presents.

He stood and tapped a fork against his glass to get everyone's attention. "Okay everyone, time for the good stuff—for Glinda, that is. Then to the *real* good stuff." He nodded to the open bar, and everyone chuckled.

I walked to the end of the table where the embarrassingly large number of gifts were piled high. "You guys shouldn't have."

Naturally, that was everyone's cue to tell me how much I deserved it. What can I say? I had nice friends. I honestly wasn't sure what to open first, so I picked up a card. "It's from Maude."

Maude Daniels ran the tea shop next door. I opened it and sucked in a breath. "It's a gift card for ten teas. Thank you. That's very generous of you."

"Nonsense. This way, you'll be sure to stop in often," she said with a smile.

How sweet, but I knew it was her code for wanting to gossip, which was fine by me. I spent the next ten minutes opening almost all of my gifts, one of which was another gift card from my favorite coffee shop, run by Maude's twin sister, Miriam. Those two were highly competitive.

Next, I picked up a pretty package wrapped in the candy store's, Broomsticks and Gumdrops, signature paper. I ripped it off. I should have saved it, but I was too excited to see what was inside. "It's from Courtney and Dominic. Thank you."

"You're welcome!"

Courtney Higgins ran the candy store, and Dominic Geno was her boyfriend. I lifted the lid and nearly gasped. Layers of chocolate ringed a pile of pink gumdrops. "This is amazing."

"Enjoy."

"Oh, I'll enjoy it all right. The hard part will be not eating it at one sitting."

The crowd laughed. The next was a gift from my cousin, Rihanna. She gave me a pink and black short-sleeved shirt, which was awesome, because pink was my signature color, and the black represented her favorite color. "I love it."

I purposefully left the two gifts from the most important people to last. I picked up the one from my parents.

"Before you open it," Mom said, "you need to know that this is from Nana."

"Nana?" My grandmother had passed away a few years ago. True, she would often show up in her ghost form at various times, but I didn't think she was able to buy something wherever witches went when they died.

"Yes. I was rooting through my closet looking for a book, when I came across this box. When I opened it, I remembered her telling me that this was for you. I'm sorry I took so long to give it to you."

"That's okay. I have it now." Anything from my grand-mother was wonderful. The only thing I had of hers was my magical pink pendant.

I tore off the pink paper to reveal a small jewelry box. When I opened it, my breath caught at the beauty of the ring. I swear the pink diamond on my necklace heated in response. I always told myself that it was my grandmother's way of letting me know she was close by.

The pink diamond in this ring was surrounded by an ornate gold setting. "It's beautiful. Do you know if it has any *special* properties?"

I was referring to magic of course. My necklace had plenty, but I didn't know about this ring.

"I never asked Mom. She just said it was for you."

Excited, I slipped it on. Before I had the chance to admire it further, something really, really strange happened. It had to be the bank of clouds floating off of the Gulf moving toward me, because there was no way I was seeing a boatload of ghosts. The issue was that while they might have been see-through like clouds, these had faces. Did clouds have eyes, a nose, and a mouth? I swore several of them were even smiling.

"Glinda?" Jaxson placed a hand on my wrist. "Are you okay?"

No, I wasn't okay. If I'd had anything to drink besides iced tea, I would have thought I was in an alcohol induced stupor. I didn't want to explain what happened for fear I'd end up making a scene. "Yeah, I'm good."

I immediately removed the ring and placed it back in its case. Like a flash, the ghosts—I mean the clouds—disappeared. That unnerved me, but I smiled anyway, trying to act as if all was well.

"You have one more to open." My boyfriend handed me a small present that looked similar to the ring box I'd just opened.

My pulse soared. *Calm down, Glinda.* If this contained an engagement ring, Jaxson would be on one knee, right? I carefully removed the pretty paper and then opened the blue velvet box. I gasped when I saw the diamond earrings. Contrary to what I'd just hoped for, I was not disappointed in the least—okay maybe just a little bit—but these earrings were spectacular. I looked up at Jaxson. "This is too much."

"Why? You deserve it, and it goes with your diamond bracelet." He nodded to what was on my wrist.

Of course, that bracelet was fake, and I imagined these earrings were not. I set the box down. "I want to try them on."

My ears were already pierced, so slipping them through the holes was easy. Once in, I looked around, posing with the bracelet.

"They are perfect," Jaxson said. "Just like you."

When I stood on my toes and kissed him, the group applauded. "You are the best," I whispered in his ear.

Jaxson leaned back and grinned. "All right everyone. Now, the real party begins."

I wanted to tell him about seeing the ghosts, but maybe that whole event had been my imagination. The ring had been a gift from my Nana, and imagining I was seeing her friends allowed me to be closer to her—if only for a few seconds.

For the next few hours, I chatted with everyone. The only two notable friends who had not come were our two gargoyle shifters. Witch's Cove sure was collecting—if that was the right word—a rather strange assortment of people, but I adored them all.

Because I was still a bit shaken from my sighting, I stuck to iced tea. If I downed a glass or two of wine, I didn't trust myself not to blab to everyone what I'd seen.

When people started to leave, I hugged each of them goodbye and thanked them for their wonderful present. When the place cleared out, I gathered my gifts as the busboys descended, whisking away the plates and glasses.

"I'll help take these up to your place," Jaxson said.

"Thanks."

Between the two of us, we managed to carry them through the restaurant and up the back staircase to my apartment. To say the least, its location was convenient. Jaxson slipped the keys from my nearly full hands and opened the door.

Iggy was there, sitting on his stool, looking out of the window. He turned to me. "How was the party?"

I couldn't tell if he was upset or not that he'd missed it, but he'd been the one to decide it was best if he stayed home. "Great, but strange."

Jaxson placed the gifts on the coffee table. "I knew something was off with you. Let me get us some coffee, and you can tell me what happened down there."

I held up a hand. "No coffee for me. I'm about to float away as it is."

"Mind if I fix a cup for myself?"

"Go ahead."

Iggy hopped off his stool and waddled after Jaxson. "Can you get me some lettuce?"

Iggy took after me—he was always hungry. I dropped onto the sofa, still trying to figure out if I was crazy or not. A few minutes later, Jaxson came out carrying a steaming mug, placed it on the nearly full table, and then sat next to me.

"Tell me what happened."

He could read me well. "Please don't think I'm losing it, but when I put on the ring from my grandmother, I saw a slew of ghosts floating around me." There. I'd said it.

"Ghosts?"

"Yes, ghosts. Sure, I've seen my share in the past, but usually it is during a séance, or if they need me to solve their murder." That had happened once or twice in the past.

"Can I see this ring?" Jaxson was probably just trying to calm me down, but I appreciated it anyway. I located the box and handed it to him.

"Don't get your hopes up. You won't see any ghosts since you're not a warlock."

"I know." He opened it, and when he lifted the ring out of the case, he froze. Jaxson looked around. "No freakin' way."

Chapter Two

"FUNNY, FUNNY. YOU don't need to humor me," I said. Jaxson looked over at me. "You don't see the ghosts?"

"No, silly. I don't see them."

He looked in the direction of the kitchen and squinted. He then stood and walked away from the sofa.

"I don't see anything, either," Iggy complained.

Jaxson turned around. Oh my, his skin had turned a rather unhealthy shade of white. I patted the seat next to me. "Maybe you should sit down."

"I think I will."

He returned to the sofa. As soon as he placed the ring back into the open box, he stilled. "They're gone."

"That's what happened to me. Are you saying you actually saw the ghosts?"

"Yes. One was even trying to talk to me, but I couldn't understand her."

Iggy crawled up onto the table. As quick as a fox, he snatched the ring and then dove off the table. I expected him to turn around and return it, but instead, he rushed to the kitchen and stopped dead in his tracks. What was he up to? I jumped into action and strode over to him. "Where are you going, young man?"

"Okay, I'll tell her," Iggy said and placed the ring on the floor before turning around.

I immediately picked it up and shoved the ring into my pocket. I wasn't in a ghostly mood anymore. However, my insatiable curiosity got the best of me. "Okay, Mr. Detective, what just happened?"

"Agnes said they are worried about your grandmother."

"Agnes? Who is Agnes?" Maybe I should pop open one of my birthday bottles of wine in hopes that the alcohol would clear things up. Iced tea sure hadn't done the trick.

"How would I know who Agnes is?" Iggy said with a way too sassy tone. "She's some ghost."

"Okay, but why was she worried about Nana?"

"She didn't say." He bobbed his head.

"Easy there, big boy." Defensive much?

Now, I was the one who had to sit down. As soon as I placed the ring in the box and closed the lid, Jaxson wrapped an arm around my shoulder and drew me close. "I saw four ghosts," he whispered.

I believed Jaxson. Iggy? Maybe not. He often just wanted to be part of the group. I wasn't saying he was lying. He could see ghosts. Heck, he saw a cat ghost when I couldn't, but did he really see *these* ghosts?

I sat up straighter. "Iggy, what did Agnes look like?"

"Why is that important?" His rather petulant tone was probably due to the fact I had interrupted his conversation. How was I to know he could see them?

Jaxson leaned over and cupped my ear so Iggy couldn't hear. "I saw two men and two women. Three had gray hair, and one of the men looked to be in his fifties. Their pale complexions made it hard to tell their age, however."

Wow. That was intense. "Iggy, I want to know if maybe this ghost was Nana's age."

"No, none of the four were *that* old."

Four? "Can you describe any of them?"

"They were ghosts, but they smelled good."

That was an odd comment. I didn't remember a scent whenever I had been involved in a ghost sighting at a séance. "Were the women wearing perfume?"

Iggy looked off to the side. "Could be, but they smelled like hibiscus flowers."

Iggy was an iguana, which meant he had a heightened sense of smell. "Anything else?"

"What more do you want to know?" He swished his tail.

I dipped my chin and gave him the sternest look I could muster. "Iggy Goodall."

"Okay, okay. All I remember is that they were as old as Aunt Fern maybe, but to me everyone looks old."

She was in her late sixties. That fit with what Jaxson said.

"Were all of them women?" Jaxson asked.

"No. Two were men."

Now I was officially freaked out. "At the party, I saw about ten of them, which means that all but four left."

"Where did they go?" Iggy asked.

"I don't know. They didn't talk to me at the party. Do you want to ask them now?" I nodded to the ring box.

"Not tonight. I'm tired. I'm hitting the hay, or rather the rattan stool."

That wasn't nice, but maybe he was a bit bothered and

didn't want to admit it. Though what teenager ever did?

While Iggy waddled off to his personal space, I turned to Jaxson. "What are you thinking?"

"Me? I think I've lost my mind. I only had one beer about an hour ago, so I am clear-headed, but I'm a human, not a warlock. I shouldn't have been able to see anything."

"The ring must be magic. It came from Nana, so it makes sense."

"Have you ever heard of a ring giving you the ability to see ghosts, though?" he asked. "The first time it happened, you had to drink some magical pink potion."

"I know. My mom must not have ever tried on the ring. If she had, she would have used it every time she wanted to talk to the dead instead of doing her candle lighting and sage ceremony." The realization of what this could mean for our sleuth business suddenly struck me. "With this ring, we can call upon a murdered victim anytime we want and ask them who killed them?"

Jaxson dragged a hand down his stubbled cheeks. "That would be something, but we both know that too often the victims don't know who killed them."

"Sure, but some of them might. Can't you see that this could be revolutionary to our company?"

Jaxson sobered. "That would be great, but don't get your hopes up. It's too good to be true. I say we wait to see what happens tomorrow. Maybe they'll return and clear things up. Or…we can ask them now." He took the ring out of the box and placed it on his palm.

As if he couldn't help himself, he looked toward the kitchen. Then he checked the rest of the apartment. "They're gone."

"What do you mean they're gone?" I had to see for my-self. I slipped the ring from his hand and placed it on my finger. I honestly expected the ghosts to be floating all around me once more, but they were nowhere to be seen. "You're right. Maybe it's late, and they had to get back."

Jaxson dipped his chin. "Really? You think ghosts have a curfew?"

I hadn't been thinking. "I suppose not."

"How about you put the ring away and then take a nice hot shower? After a good night's sleep, tomorrow we can delve into this very strange phenomenon."

I wrapped my arms around his neck. "You are the best. Thank you."

He leaned forward and kissed me. Jaxson then got up. "Don't worry, we will figure this out."

"I hope so."

"CAN I TOUCH the ring again?" Iggy asked.

He was sitting on my bed—a place where he wasn't sup-posed to be—especially when I was trying to sleep. "No, now let me get some much needed shuteye."

"Ah, you're a bit backward. It's time to get up."

"What time is it?"

"Ten a.m." Believe it or not, Iggy could read, but he could only tell time if the clock was digital.

How could it be morning? I'd just gone to bed. I blew out a breath and sat up. "Why does turning twenty-eight make me feel old?"

"Who knows? Who cares? Just get up. We have to figure out the ghosts. What if they show up today and you're still in your pajamas?"

Iggy sometimes could be rather logical. "Okay. Get off the bed so I can get dressed."

Once he crawled back to the floor, I dragged myself into the bathroom, turned on the shower, and undressed. I checked the mirror to see if by some chance my grandmother had left me a message. Even though it had happened once before, nothing was there now. Darn. I could really use her guidance.

When the water heated, I hopped in the shower and cleaned up. The billowing steam would allow any mirror message to show. After I finished and stepped in front of the sink, I was disappointed to find nothing but a fogged up mirror. Oh, well. Maybe Nana decided to contact me via her friends instead. But why? Was she injured or too weak to chat? I had always assumed dead people couldn't get sick or grow older.

As quickly as I could, I dressed. Since it was late, I decided to grab coffee at the office instead of getting a to-go cup downstairs at the restaurant.

For a change, Iggy was waiting by my purse when I stepped into the living room. "I see you're raring to go."

"I've been up for hours. You're the lazy one."

That's because he often dozed during the day. "Whatever."

With Iggy in tow, I walked over to the office, which was only two buildings away. When I stepped into our main room, Jaxson was at his desk, and my nineteen-year-old cousin was looking through photos on her camera. She must have risen at the crack of dawn to take them.

"Hey, all," I said.

"Did you really see ghosts?" Rihanna sounded really excited.

"We all did." I set down my purse. "Unless I dreamt it."

Jaxson shook his head. "You didn't."

"Can I see the ring? Did you bring it?" she asked.

"I did. I thought I might try again to contact them." I removed the ring from my purse and handed her the box. "When you put it on, tell me what you see. I'm curious if it is the same as what Jaxson and Iggy saw."

Rihanna inhaled as she took the box and opened it. "It's so pretty."

"Isn't it though?"

"Here goes." Rihanna slipped on the ring and then looked up, her eyes sparkling with anticipation. She visually searched the entire room, saying nothing.

"Do you see them?"

"No. No one is here. Maybe I don't have the power to see these ghosts, even though I've seen Nana."

That can't be. She was a witch. "Let me try."

Rihanna removed the ring and handed it to me. Once I put it on, I expected to be once more surrounded by ghosts, only no one was there. That's the second time I'd failed.

"Well?" she asked.

"They really are gone. Maybe they had to leave last night." I didn't know whether to rejoice or be disappointed.

"Maybe they only came for your birthday," Iggy said.

"Maybe, but the ring was Nana's. If she asked my mom to give it to me, she must have wanted me to see those ghosts. You said that Agnes told you that they were worried about Nana, right?"

"Yes." Iggy moved closer. "Let me try. I'm more special than you."

He was indeed special, but more than the rest of us? That was debatable. "Fine. You did see that cat ghost, and I didn't."

I placed the ring on the coffee table, and Iggy slipped as much of his claw through the opening as he could. As he did a visual sweep of the room, his chest slowly lowered. I recognized what that body language meant—he hadn't seen anything either.

"I got squat," he announced.

"That's okay. Iggy, did Agnes tell you her last name or how she knew Nana?"

"No and no. You didn't give me enough time to ask for introductions. Remember?"

I had rushed over the moment he had reached the kitchen. "Sorry."

I should have paid more attention to all of my grandmother's friends, but I had been too preoccupied with school and working to spend time with them. "I'll ask Aunt Fern if she knows anything about someone named Agnes. That might give me a hint as to what is going on. Anyone up for some breakfast at the Tiki Hut?" I asked.

"I ate earlier, but I could use another cup of coffee," Jaxson said.

"Ditto, but I'll join you." Rihanna chimed in.

Iggy would want to go in order not to be left behind.

"Let's go."

As we entered the Tiki Hut Grill, it occurred to me that maybe ghosts didn't like daylight—kind of like vampires. Ooh, vampire ghosts. Were there such things?

"Something funny?" Jaxson asked.

I told him about vampire ghosts. "I don't think they exist, but I didn't think gargoyle shifters existed either until I met two of them. So maybe vampire ghosts are real."

Iggy poked his head out of my bag. "I hope they aren't. One of them could bite me and turn me into an iguana vampire."

I chuckled. "No, silly. A ghost couldn't do that." Or so I believed. "I think I need to monitor what television shows you're watching."

"You wouldn't dare."

I didn't respond. Let him stew about that.

Since Aunt Fern was cashing someone out at the counter, I waved to Penny who was working today and then headed over to her section.

"Hey, birthday girl. How are you feeling?"

I didn't have a hangover if that was why she asked. "Good, but I would like to talk with you when you have a moment."

"Sure. Take table two. I'll be right back."

We sat down and waited for Penny to return. Having worked here for three years, I didn't need to look at the menu. She came back carrying an order pad.

"What can I get you all?"

We ordered, and I added some lettuce for Iggy. "Are you and Hunter free for dinner?"

She cocked her head. "Sure, what's up?"

"I'd rather tell you later. Is tonight good?"

"It's perfect. Mom is watching Tommy."

Tommy was her nine-year-old son. "Let's meet here at eight if that's not too late."

Penny's brows rose. I rarely ate that late, but there was a reason for the request. "I'll call Hunter and get back to you."

"Perfect." Once Penny left, I turned to Rihanna and Jaxson. Iggy was still in my bag, probably afraid the vampires would get him. Though I couldn't believe he thought they would be solid enough to bite anything. "Do you think it's possible that these ghosts only come out when it is dark?"

Jaxson looked at my cousin and then back at me. "It makes sense, but if you recall, they disappeared last *night*."

"I know, but maybe they only had so much energy to be seen."

Jaxson shrugged.

"It's a reasonable assumption," Rihanna said.

I noticed that my aunt was free, so I motioned her to join us. She might know something about who Agnes was.

She wiped her hands on her apron and came over. "How does it feel to be twenty-eight?" she asked.

Why were people so obsessed with age? Sheesh. "It's only been one day."

Aunt Fern smiled. "I hope it's a good one."

Enough of the small talk. I motioned she take the fourth chair. "I had a sighting last night."

She leaned forward. "You saw a ghost?" I nodded. "Who?"

I explained about putting on Nana's ring at the party and seeing a ton of them. "Back at the apartment, both Jaxson and

Iggy touched the ring, and they each saw four ghosts."

"Jaxson saw ghosts? How can that be?"

"I don't know. It has to be the ring. Today, when we tried, no one showed up. I thought maybe some ghosts only like the night."

"Not my Harold. He was here during the day all the time."

That was true. I'd forgotten about that. "One of the ghosts told Iggy that her name was Agnes and that they were worried about Nana. Do you recall my grandmother having any friend by that name?"

"Agnes? Hmm. Your grandmother was older than me, but I do recall an Agnes Lochridge. She died quite a few years before your grandmother, though."

"That could be her. I'll check it out. Thank you." As much as I wanted to pick her brain, two couples had queued up at the counter. "You have some customers."

Aunt Fern reached out and squeezed my hand. "Keep me in the loop."

"I will."

Once she left, I turned to Jaxson. "Do you think your brother and Andorra can join us for dinner tonight, assuming they are free?"

"I can ask, but what do you think they can do?"

"I need help with a plan."

"Then sure," he said.

Our meals arrived, and with it the news that Hunter was available tonight. "We'll meet you here at eight," Penny said.

"I'm looking forward to it."

Jaxson pulled out his phone. "Let me check if Drake and

Andorra can join us."

His brother's wine and cheese shop was closed on Sunday, so unless Drake and Andorra had other plans, there was no reason why they couldn't come.

Jaxson gave him a call and told him that I needed to do some brainstorming, though he wasn't specific as to its nature. He nodded and then smiled. "Great. Meet us at eight at the Tiki Hut." He disconnected and placed his phone on the table. "It's all set."

I turned to Rihanna. "Do you think Gavin will want to join us?"

"I'm sure he would, but he left this morning for school. Classes start on Tuesday."

"I'm sorry. Can you come?"

She smiled. "I'd love to."

Iggy popped his head up out of my purse and stared at me. "You waiting to engrave an invitation for me? I was the one who actually spoke with Agnes, you know."

I swallowed a laugh. "If you aren't too busy, Mr. Detective, would you like to join us for dinner?"

"Nah, I'm going out with Aimee."

My familiar was a real stinker. "Fine. Have fun."

"Or I could cancel and go out with her another time?"

"Don't bother." Iggy was a manipulator and whenever possible, I tried to nip that bad habit in the bud.

He lifted his head. "See if I tell you what Agnes says the next time I see her."

Iggy could no more resist telling me than he could fly. "We'll see about that."

Chapter Three

"I CAN'T BELIEVE you saw so many ghosts," Hunter said. "How cool is that?"

"I brought the ring if you want to try it." I wiggled my eyebrows in invitation.

"Here?" He looked around the rather full restaurant. "I'm not saying I'd freak out if I saw something like that, but who knows? Maybe I would."

Hunter would never lose his cool, but Penny might, even though she was a witch and knew ghosts existed. He probably was trying to protect her. "You might be right. Maybe after we finish eating, we can all head to the beach and pass the ring around."

"That's a better idea," he said. "We don't need a crowd."

Andorra sipped her drink. "Are you going to check out Agnes Lochridge?"

"If I can find her—well, not her specifically, since she's dead—but maybe some of her friends."

"What do you hope to learn?" Jaxson asked.

"I don't know. That's why I called on these guys. I can't let this drop. I'm sure the ghosts must be connected to Nana in some way. If they weren't, they wouldn't have said they were worried about her."

"What did Gertrude say?" Andorra asked.

"I haven't spoken with her, though I plan to. Do you know if either Genevieve or Hugo have had any experience with ghosts?"

Those two were only part human even though they looked like humans when they weren't in their stone gargoyle form—it was complicated, like relationships.

"I've never asked them. Clearly, I'm not the best of hosts."

Drake clasped her hand. "You can't say that. You only reunited with Hugo recently."

"True."

As for Genevieve, she just showed up in her shifted human form about a month ago and had demonstrated extensive talents. I had no idea if these abilities extended to the other side—or whatever you called the place where witches and warlocks crossed over. Whenever Nana had appeared of late, she would deliver her message and disappear. She wasn't one to stick around and have long conversations about her life in the hereafter.

"I should probably ask my mom what her thoughts are about the afterlife. Quite often, she speaks to those who've passed over, but I don't know if she's ever asked them what it's like up there," I said.

"I bet Gertrude knows." My cousin and Gertrude shared a psychic connection, which might be one of the reasons why Rihanna was such a big fan of hers, like I was.

"When I speak with Gertrude tomorrow, I'll ask her about the afterlife, but I want to do a little checking on this Agnes Lochridge first."

"I can ask Gavin's mom if she can look into the morgue

records to see how this woman died," Rihanna said. "Assuming she was autopsied."

"That would be great."

Once the topic of the ghosts was exhausted, we moved on to Hunter's job as a forest ranger. I was always interested in what it was like to be in the forest all day, especially after the clan of evil werewolves had shown up. This clan from up north came to Witch's Cove wanting to learn how Hunter and some others seemed to be immune to shifting during the full moon. That investigation resulted in several deaths—the newcomers.

"Have you come across any more of your *kind* in the woods?" I asked him.

"No, thank goodness. Except for a random small bear, some deer, a few families of raccoons, and an occasional bobcat or panther, we don't get a lot of animals—at least none that pose any threats to people. That's assuming, of course, the visitors don't leave food out."

"Good to know."

After we finished eating and had settled the bill, I invited everyone to join me on the beach. It was finally dark, and I was hoping the ghosts would appear again.

As we neared the water's edge, Andorra lifted her face to the sky and sighed. "It's so pretty out here."

"I've lived on the water my whole life," Drake said, "and yet I don't take the time to enjoy the ocean." He pointed to the shimmery surface. "Look how the moonlight skims across the water."

I inhaled, letting the salty breeze kiss my face. "It's beautiful."

As soon as I answered, I realized he was probably addressing Andorra. Whoops. Drake and I had been inseparable since middle school. It was only after Jaxson returned to Witch's Cove that things changed.

I pulled the ring from my pocket and handed the box to my cousin. "Why don't you give it a try?"

"Me?"

"You've yet to see them, and I'd love to hear your reaction."

She sucked in a deep breath. "Okay, here goes. I hope it works this time." Rihanna opened the box and slipped on the ring. Immediately, she reached out and clasped my upper arm. "Hello? Yes? How can we help you?"

Clearly, the ghosts were here, but it was a shame we all couldn't see them. I placed my hand on top of hers, making sure to touch the ring. Instantly, I saw the ghosts too. Yes!

"Hi, I'm Glinda and this is Rihanna. We're Amelia's granddaughters."

Like Jaxson and Iggy had claimed, there were four of them—two women and two men. I wondered why Nana didn't want to appear and tell us herself what was bothering her?

"It's so nice to meet Amelia's granddaughters. She talks about you two all the time," the shorter of the two women said.

"Wow. That's nice to hear." Who knew it was such a social scene up there?

"I guess you're curious to know who we are."

"That's an understatement." I wanted to know their names, why they were there, how they were able to just show up, and what connection they had to Nana. And that didn't begin to scratch the surface of my questions. The whole concept of life after death was a big black hole to me.

I had so many things to ask, but I was too stunned to form the words. Jaxson wrapped an arm around my waist and immediately stiffened.

"Hi, I'm Jaxson."

It appeared as if the other lady stepped closer—or rather floated toward him. "Well aren't you a sight for sore eyes, young man. Considering your age, I guess you have no intention of visiting us any time soon?"

"No, ma'am. Glinda needs me here."

"That's a shame, but when you come, we'll have to get together."

Was she actually hitting on Jaxson? No way. This ghost must have assumed he was a warlock because he could see her.

Once our other four friends realized that Jaxson could see them by touching me, Drake clasped Rihanna's hand, and Andorra took his. Then Penny grabbed Jaxson's free hand, and Hunter clasped hers.

"Hello, all you lovely young people. My name is Agnes Lochridge," the first women said. "Next to me is Gladys Chipper. We gave her that name since she's always so happy." The other woman smiled and waved. "Next to Gladys is Neil Phillips, and on my right is Wes Armstrong."

I didn't know if I could remember all of those names since my hands were shaking, and my mind was spinning. "Why are you worried about our grandmother?"

"A friend of hers is missing, and Amelia has been looking everywhere for her."

That sounded like Nana. "Maybe we can help. What is her name?"

"Irene."

No one said anything for a moment.

"We have to go now," the younger of the two men said. If I didn't know better, I'd say he sounded embarrassed, though I had no idea why he should be.

"Wait! We'd like to ask you a few questions," I blurted.

"You know how to find us." And then they were gone—or at least they were for me.

"Does anyone still see them?" I asked.

"No," my friends said in unison.

As if my legs could no longer hold me up, I released my grip on the ring, crossed my feet, and slipped down to sit cross-legged on the soft sand. I turned to Rihanna. "I hope you remembered their names?"

"Some." She pulled out her phone and typed something. "I got Agnes Lochridge, Gladys Chipper, though that's not her real name, Wes something, and I can't remember the other guy's name."

I racked my brain. Bob? Jack? None rang a bell. "Art?"

"No, I would have remembered that."

"It was Neil Phillips," Iggy said, who appeared out of nowhere. He must have spotted us sitting on the beach and decided to join the party. "And they say my brain isn't as big as a human's? Shows what they know."

"You're right. His name was Neil." I refused to comment on Iggy's response about being smarter than the rest of us. "Thank you, but how could you see them?"

"My tail was touching Andorra's foot."

29

VELLA DAY

"I was wondering what that was," she said.

"Iggy come sit next to me." I didn't need him scaring off the ghosts should they return. I turned around so that my back was to the ocean and then scooted away from the group. The rest formed a circle.

"Did we really see ghosts?" Drake asked in disbelief.

"I know I did," Andorra said.

"Me, too," Penny said.

Hunter kept looking around, the moonlight bathing his face. "They're gone, Hunter," I said.

"I know, but I can't figure out where the pine scent is coming from."

I sniffed the air, but could only detect salt, sand, and some perfume. "Maybe the pine scent is coming off your clothes. You were in the forest all day."

"I showered and changed. Besides, I never wear these clothes to work."

"I smelled hibiscus flowers again," Iggy said.

I tried to put the two concepts together. "For those of you who can't hear Iggy, he said that both times the ghosts have appeared, he smelled hibiscus flowers." Not that they had much of a scent to humans.

"It must be an animal thing," Jaxson said. "Both Iggy and Hunter are sort of animals."

"True." I wasn't sure how that helped, but I catalogued the information.

"What do we do now?" Hunter asked.

I appreciated his calm demeanor. "About the only person who might know something is our esteemed psychic, Gertrude Poole, though her grandson and his coven might be willing to do some research for us." He claimed I gave them the best assignments.

"Would you like us to find out about these other ghosts?" Andorra asked.

I looked over at Jaxson, and he shrugged. "Sure, the more information the better."

"What should we try to find out about them?" Andorra asked.

"How about if any of these ghosts knew Nana while she lived in Witch's Cove?"

"And Irene?" Penny asked. "Do you know anything about her?"

"No, but I'm hoping we can contact these ghosts again and ask for a last name. If I thought doing a séance to contact Nana would help, I'd conduct one. For now, we have to search for people who knew these ghosts—when they were alive, of course." I looked around. "I'll ask about Irene. Penny, do you think you can find out about Agnes Lochridge?"

"Absolutely."

"And Jaxson, do you mind taking Neil Phillips?"

"No problem."

"What about Drake and me?" Hunter asked.

"Why don't you two find out more on Wes. If any of these people lived in Witch's Cove, there has to be a record of them someplace. Naturally, I'll pick Gertrude's brain."

"Does anyone remember Wes' last name?" Drake asked.

"Armstrong, I think," Jaxson said.

"Thanks."

"Besides asking our two extraordinary gargoyle shifters what they can and can't do regarding ghosts, how about I check out Gladys Chipper—or whatever her real name is?" Andorra offered.

"Perfect."

"How can I help?" Rihanna asked.

"Would you be willing to come with me to Gertrude's tomorrow? I'm sure she'll give us some leads."

"I'd like that."

Iggy thumped his tale on my leg but didn't say anything. I knew he was waiting for his assignment. "I'll ask Iggy to be the keeper of the ring. While we are around town trying to find information, he can periodically try to contact these ghosts." I looked down at my familiar. "Are you up for that?"

"Are you kidding? I have the most important job."

"You're right about that."

"WHAT BRINGS YOU here today?" Gertrude Poole asked. Actually, I was surprised that she had to ask about our agenda since she and Rihanna had a strong mental connection. If Rihanna thought something, Gertrude knew about it.

She faced me and then motioned we sit around the coffee table. From what I'd been able to piece together, she was about ninety, though she would never tell us her exact age.

I pulled out Nana's ring that Iggy begrudgingly let me take from him this morning and placed it on the coffee table between us. Of course, I had to agree to let him tag along today. "This was my birthday present from my grandmother."

I thought about warning her that touching it could have consequences, but I wanted to see what happened when the great psychic got her hands on it.

Gertrude opened the box and studied the ring. Just as she was about to remove it, Iggy crawled out of my bag and onto the table. "Don't touch it!"

Gertrude stilled. "Why not, Iggy?"

"It's magic."

She studied him. "Magic is wonderful."

"This ring makes you see ghosts. Let me test it out first."

Before I could stop him, Iggy placed his claw on the ring. He looked around. "They still won't show up. Grr."

I almost smiled at his cute act of frustration. "I'm getting the sense that they only appear when they want to," I said.

"May I try?" Gertrude's interest must have been piqued.

"Certainly. We normally see four at a time."

"Four? Oh, my. That is unusual."

She lifted the ring off the table and then pressed it against her palm. When she closed her eyes, I thought it rather odd, but who was I to comment on the great Gertrude Poole's methods?

A moment later, she sagged and then opened them. "I could feel their power, but I didn't see anyone."

I turned to Iggy. "Did you smell hibiscus flowers just now?"

He lifted his head and sniffed. "Maybe a little."

I explained how Hunter, a werewolf, smelled pine when the ghosts first showed up, while Iggy smelled his favorite scent. I also told her that Hunter, Drake, and Jaxson had seen the ghosts, despite not being warlocks.

"That is fascinating, and you say this is from Amelia?"

"Yes."

"Did these ghosts say what they wanted?"

"Agnes Lochridge did most of the talking. She only said they were worried about Nana, but she didn't explain why, other than to say that Irene, one of Nana's friends, was missing. Do you know anything about Agnes Lochridge or who Irene is?"

Her eyes widened and then a smile filled her face. "I remember Agnes. She was Amelia's widowed friend."

"And Irene?"

"I only knew the name. Nothing more."

"Thanks. And what about Neil Phillips, Wes Armstrong, or Gladys Chipper?"

"Wes Armstrong." She smiled. "Now he was a looker."

"He knew Nana then?"

"Yes. He was friends with your grandfather."

My mother didn't speak much about her dad, because he'd passed when she was a teenager. "And Gladys?"

"I don't recall anyone by that name, but people move away from here, get married, and change their name."

Who changed their first name when they married? I doubt there were many women named Gladys in our small town, even back then, which implied she might not have lived nearby.

"What do you know about the afterlife?" I asked.

She smiled. "Are you asking if I've visited?"

What was she talking about? "No, of course not, but you've done a lot of séances. I thought maybe the topic of what goes on up there has come up."

She shook her head. "Clients don't care about that."

I could understand that. "Fine. How do you suggest we

go about helping Nana find her friend?"

"We could try contacting her, but you know Amelia; she is a stubborn one."

I looked over at Rihanna and then down at Iggy. "What do you both think?"

"You should wear the ring all the time," Rihanna said. "The ghosts seem to come when they need something. Nana will probably do the same."

"You might be right." I turned to Gertrude. "If you remember anything about these ghosts, can you let me know?"

"Why, of course."

We hugged her goodbye, and once we stepped outside, I turned to Rihanna. "You up for some diner food?"

My cousin grinned. "You mean some Dolly gossip?"

"You read my mind."

Chapter Four

DOLLY ANDREWS WAVED to us as we walked into the diner. It was lunchtime, but the place was not as crowded as it usually was this time of day, which meant the owner might have time to chat.

I wasn't all that hopeful that she'd know all or even any of the ghosts since Dolly was a lot younger than my grandmother, but it was worth asking. The ones Gertrude didn't know, might not have been from around here.

"Ladies." Dolly turned to me. "How does it feel to be twenty-eight, Glinda?"

Her, too? Or was she asking because it had been a long time since she'd been that young? "Good, but something happened at the party last night that I'd like to ask you about."

She grinned and slid in next to Rihanna. "You are a lifesaver, girl. The gossip tree has all but dried up. Tell me something good."

"I heard that a woman by the name of Irene is missing."

Dolly looked down at the table for a moment probably trying to dig through her memories. "Irene? What's her last name?"

I was hoping she wouldn't ask. "I don't know. You haven't heard of anyone disappearing of late?"

She shook her head. "No, and Irene isn't a real common name these days."

"What about Agnes Lochridge? Did you know her?" I realize that Penny was going to ask about her, but with her busy schedule, she might not have time to get to Dolly.

"That name sounds familiar, but I can't say from where. Why don't you ask Pearl? If anyone knows, it will be her."

"That's a great idea. By any chance have you heard of Wes Armstrong?"

She pressed her lips together. "Sorry. Are you sure these people are from Witch's Cove?"

"Wes was."

"Was?"

This was going to be hard to explain. "I think he's passed on."

"That's a shame, but as I said, Pearl is your best bet."

"We will definitely talk with her."

"Anything else?" Dolly asked.

She was asking if we had any more gossip, but I wasn't ready to tell her about my sightings. The fewer people who knew about the ghosts, the better—at least for now. "Just a coffee and a BLT."

"You got it. And for you, Rihanna?"

"A coffee and a grilled cheese."

"That's usually Glinda's go-to meal."

"It doesn't hurt to switch things up," Rihanna said with a smile.

She was right. "And some lettuce for you know who?" I glanced to my purse.

"Of course. Be right back."

Once Dolly returned to the kitchen, I leaned forward. "This might be harder than I thought. Agnes might not look too terribly old, but if she died before Nana, she could be close to ninety by now if she were alive."

"I hadn't thought of that."

It wasn't long before Dolly delivered our meal. "I just had to call Pearl and tell her. She says she remembers Agnes and is happy to talk with you about her."

I chuckled. "You are the best."

"I try."

In relative silence, we chowed down our meal since I needed a moment to figure out how much to tell Pearl. I feared if I asked about a missing person that she'd tell the sheriff, who then might waste valuable time on a wild goose chase. No telling where Irene lived.

After we finished and paid, we walked across the street and found Pearl talking with Nash. When she spotted us, she smiled and came over. "Hello, ladies. Don't tell me you're here to report a crime?"

I thought Dolly had told her our agenda. Or did the crime involve a missing person? "Do you have a minute to chat?"

Her eyes shone. "I always have time for some gossip. Dolly called and said you needed some help. Is that right?"

Even though the sheriff's grandmother was close to eighty, she was usually quite sharp, despite being a little hard of hearing. Today? Maybe not so much. "Yes. Dolly said you knew an Agnes Lochridge?"

"Agnes? Sure, though we weren't good friends. She died a

while ago, though. Why?"

"I had this strange dream about her. I didn't know her, but she said she was friends with my grandmother."

"She was. Both were widows, so they were quite close."

That meant my mom might remember Agnes. "How did Agnes die?"

"Hmm. I can't remember, but maybe the medical examiner would have something in her files."

If it was from natural causes, there might not have been an autopsy. Rihanna said she'd check. "I'll look into it. Have you heard of Wes Armstrong?"

She stiffened. "Boy have I. The man was a real womanizer. He was after your grandmother something fierce, but she never gave him the time of day," Pearl said with pride.

Wow. I guess that was a good thing, though I couldn't really picture my grandmother being someone men sought out. However, she was a witch, and if Wes Armstrong was now in the same place as Nana, he might be a warlock. That was based on the assumption that people with magical abilities ended up in the same place.

"Good to know. Thanks. Any idea who Neil Phillips is?"

"Hmm. I've never heard of him, but why are you asking about these people? That dream must have been some doozy."

I should have anticipated she'd wonder. Should I tell Pearl the truth? I was well aware she'd eventually tell everyone what I saw, but I needed her help. Decisions, decisions.

While Pearl wasn't a witch, she was well aware that I was. "Don't mention it to Steve, but do you remember the ring my mom gave me last night that belonged to my grandmother?" I held out my hand to show off my present.

She studied it. "Of course. It's beautiful."

"Thanks. When I first put it on, four ghosts appeared, all claiming to be worried about my grandmother." That wasn't exactly how it happened, but it was close enough.

"Four ghosts? What did they say?"

"Not much. They introduced themselves and then disappeared."

"Give me their names, and I'll see what I can find out about them."

I appreciated that she didn't question my ghost sighting, though I shouldn't be all that surprised. Pearl knew I'd seen ghosts several times in the past. In hindsight, I probably should have put her on the case right away. I listed the four names. "Anything you learn will be helpful, but do me a favor?"

"Sure."

"For the moment, don't tell people about my ghost sighting. It's a little embarrassing."

"My lips are sealed."

I doubted that, but I thanked her again anyway. Once outside, I turned to Rihanna. "How about we stop by to see if Mom knows anything? If these ghosts were friends of Nana's, Mom might have met them."

"Good idea."

Iggy popped his head up. "I don't like going there."

That came as a surprise. "Why not?"

"Hel-lo? That evil dog bit me the last time, and I have the scar to prove it."

To clarify, it was merely a small scratch from Toto's paw. "Watch it. That Cairn Terrier is my mother's pride and joy.

Besides, Toto weighs less than you. I bet she's afraid of you, not the other way around." Iggy had probably tormented poor Toto until she had to retaliate.

"I don't like all that shrill yapping either. It hurts my ears. Not to mention, it smells in there."

"It's the embalming room that you don't like, but fine. I'll drop you off at the office." Sheesh. Spoil him much?

Once Iggy was on his way up the railing leading to our office, Rihanna and I went next door to the funeral home. I usually loved the scent of flowers, but Iggy was right. The smell was a bit overpowering today. Lilies carried such a strong fragrance.

"Let's check Mom's office. I bet she's in there." I knocked on the slightly open door, went in, and found her at her computer.

She looked up and smiled. "This is a nice surprise. What brings you girls here?" Mom stood and hugged us both.

Rihanna and I each pulled up a chair. Since Toto wasn't around, I figured Dad must be taking her for her afternoon walk. "I had a reaction to Nana's ring."

I waved my hand to show her I was wearing it.

"What kind of reaction?"

I went through the whole series of events starting with how I saw several ghosts when I first tried on the ring. I explained that Rihanna put on the ring when a group of us went to the beach last night. "When we held hands, everyone saw four ghosts."

"Did they all have magical abilities?"

I assumed she meant the people and not the ghosts. "No."

"I've never heard of anything like that."

41

"Me neither," I said. "I figured the ring was very magical."

"Was Nana one of the ghosts?"

What? She didn't want to find out more about this ring? Or did she know about it already and didn't feel like sharing? My mom had many of the same traits as Nana—being closed-mouthed was but one of them.

"No." I told her about the four ghosts who'd shown up, and that Agnes Lochridge was worried about Nana. "Do you know anything about any of them?"

"This is a lot to take in," my mom said. "But sure, I knew Agnes. She and your grandmother were close."

"When did she die?" Pearl claimed it was several years before Nana passed, but a more accurate time frame would be helpful.

"I'm not good at keeping dates in my head, but if I had to guess, I'd say about three years before your grandmother."

"Thanks. They were on good terms, right?" I had no idea why I asked that since Mom said they were close, but something seemed off to me.

"Yes, except near the end."

"Why at the end?"

"Let's say that Agnes engaged in some unscrupulous activities with a man, and Mom didn't approve."

"Was that man Wes Armstrong?" I asked, hope welling within.

"No." Her lips pressed together.

I recognized those pursed lips. It meant no more information would be forthcoming today. Clearly, something had gone on. For now, I'd let it drop. "Final question. Do you know who Irene is?"

"Irene? Oh, yes."

My pulse soared. "Who?"

"If you're talking about Nana's friend, Irene, that's Irene Talbert."

The name didn't ring a bell. "Does she still live in town?"

"Irene? Oh, no. She died many years ago, too."

"She's dead? Are you sure?"

"I prepared her myself since the funeral was held here."

"Wow, but if she's dead, why would Nana say that Irene is missing?" I asked.

"I don't know, sweetie. Can you use the ring to contact Mom?"

"You know Nana. She only shows up when she wants to."

My mother nodded. "How well I know. I've tried on and off to connect with her, but she's hard to get a hold of. Maybe Pearl knows Irene."

"I'm glad to know Nana is such a socialite, but I'll definitely ask Pearl again now that I have her last name." This might be the clue I needed. "Thanks." I held up a finger. "One more thing. Let me ask you. What do you know about the afterlife?"

"I don't know what you mean?"

"Since Agnes claimed a friend of Nana's is missing, either your mother is losing it, or this friend was able to sneak out, not that I can imagine what that would entail exactly."

"You know full well that your grandmother is sharp as a tack."

Every time Nana had appeared, she imparted good information. "I know. You're right. Do you believe ghosts can just leave when they want to? I mean, I understand if there is a séance in which they are summoned, they might show up, but how can those four ghosts just appear without being contacted?"

My mom stared at me for a bit. "You really think I'd know?"

"You talk to the dead frequently."

"True, but I don't ask them about their accommodations or the rules and regulations of where they are. Furthermore, I don't know if all people who have passed over end up in the same place. I kind of assumed that people of magic go to one place and the regular folks go someplace else, but that's just a guess, or maybe I should say, a hope."

"That was my thought, too. The next time Nana appears, I'll ask her." Not that she'd necessarily tell me. They might have had to sign some kind of non-disclosure contract when they arrive. How they would accomplish that if they couldn't move a pen, I don't know.

"Tell me what she says," Mom said.

"Will do." As soon as we walked out, I turned to Rihanna. "What do you think?"

"Do I think someone escaped this witch Nirvana place?"

I chuckled. "Kind of. But escaping implies there would be walls and maybe sentries."

"I doubt there are walls. Why have them if ghosts can go through solid objects?"

"You know this, how?" I asked.

"I realize that Genevieve isn't a ghost, but she can teleport through walls, so why can't ghosts do the same thing? And think about it. When we do a séance, it's not like the dead hop on a plane to get here. They just appear out of thin air.

They have to have the ability to go through walls since I've never seen the office door open and then close, have you?"

"No." I think my birthday was having more of an effect on me than I realized. "I need an iced tea to clear the cobwebs from my brain. Want to join me?"

She smiled. "You think Maude might know something, don't you?"

I could never fool her. "Not about the afterlife but perhaps about our four ghosts."

"We should let Jaxson know," she said. "He might have some information on Neil Phillips by now."

I smiled. "I like the way you think."

I called him as we headed to the tea shop. "Hey, Rihanna and I are on our way to Maude's. Want to join us?"

"Sure, but give me two minutes. I'm just finishing up with something."

"I'll save you a seat." I disconnected. "He's coming."

The tea shop was surprisingly crowded. The combination of cinnamon, cloves, and some unidentifiable spices made my stomach grumble.

I looked around. All of the tables near the windows were taken, so we grabbed one at the rear of the store. Considering our conversation would be about ghosts, it might be best to remain a little isolated.

Because the server was super busy, Jaxson arrived before she or Maude came over to take our order. He slid in across from me. "Did you ladies find out anything?"

"We did. For starters, we learned that Irene's last name is Talbert."

His eyebrows rose. "That's a good start. Where does she

live?"

"She's dead."

His chin tucked in. "Are you sure? I thought your grandmother was looking for her."

Rihanna turned to me. "I know what Aunt Wendy said, but I think Nana might be starting to lose it."

"How can she?" I whispered. "She doesn't have a body. When a person dies, they can't *lose* anything anymore—or be in any pain."

"Do you really know what goes on up there?" Rihanna motioned upward with her eyes.

"No, but I suppose if someone had a near death experience, they might have an idea. I've never had one nor has Mom."

Just then Maude came over looking a little frazzled. "Sorry, I didn't see you come in. Today has been crazy."

"Any idea why?"

"It's hot, maybe? I don't know."

"Before we order, can I ask you a question?"

"Sure."

"Do you know an Irene Talbert? I realize she's passed, but did you know her?"

"Irene?" Maude pulled up a chair. This must be good. "Why, yes I did."

"Tell me."

"Well, the official statement is that Irene was killed by some random hit-and-run driver."

I didn't see that one coming. "What's the unofficial statement?"

"It was intentional."

"She was murdered?" I wanted to be certain I understood.

"Yes."

"Who ran her over?" Rihanna asked.

"That I don't know. Some think it was her husband, Adam, but I didn't know him. Actually, I didn't know Irene all that well either."

For being not very familiar with the victim, she was a wealth of information. "I assume Adam is dead, too?"

"I haven't heard that he's gone, but that doesn't mean he's still alive. Last report, he was in Belleview in a mental hospital. He's old, so he could have died already. Why the sudden interest?"

I wasn't about to say my grandmother thought Irene, a dead woman, was missing. Maude would say she was crazy. "Someone mentioned her name, and I was curious."

"Uh-huh."

Darn. I shouldn't be surprised that she saw right through me. "Okay, okay. I'm working on something. It's not a case, exactly, but it's something I need to see through."

Jaxson placed a hand over Maude's. "We'll tell you if we learn anything important."

Maude tilted her head and looked at Jaxson adoringly. He seemed to have that effect on women—especially the older females. "Thank you."

"May we order?" I asked. "I need something to help me think."

"Oh, my yes." She pushed back her chair and stood. "Tell me what you want."

I had the coupons for the teas, but I'd left them at my apartment. I'd be sure to remember to bring one the next time. "I'll have my usual sweet, iced tea and a blueberry muffin."

"You got it."

Rihanna and Jaxson ordered, and as soon as Maude returned to the counter, I faced Jaxson. "Did you find out anything about Neil Phillips?"

"Sadly, no, which leads me to believe he's not from here."

"I guess there is no reason to assume he has to be. I imagine once you pass over, you could meet a ton of people from anywhere." Or at least I wanted to think it was wonderful like that.

"Are we going to visit Irene's husband next?" Rihanna asked.

Chapter Five

"I DEFINITELY WANT to look for Adam Talbert, assuming he is still alive," I said.

"Even if he is," Jaxson said, "he's in a mental institution. Can you rely on anything he tells you?"

I leaned back in my seat. "You sure have a way to cheer up a girl."

He grinned. "Just trying to help. What I will do is find out the location of this hospital in Belleview and give them a call."

Belleview was only about an hour's drive from here. "That would be wonderful. Thank you."

"How long do you think Penny and Andorra will take with their assignments?" Rihanna asked.

"I'm sure Andorra and Penny will call as soon as they learn anything, though I don't know what else we need to find out about Agnes. I would, however, like to know what Genevieve and Hugo have to say. I'm really hoping they have a secret way to connect to the dead—as in talk to the ghosts whenever they want."

Jaxson's brows rose. "Have you heard that familiars can do this? Iggy sure can't."

"I know, but gargoyles seem to have many different talents." He nodded. "Who knew they could teleport or extinguish fires?"

"Good point."

Rihanna tapped the table with her finger. "Change of subject. You know, if Irene was in a hit-and-run accident, I'm sure there will be newspaper articles about it, or at the very least, there should be records at the morgue regarding the injuries to her body. I'm not sure how that will help us, but it might. Since I plan to speak with Elissa about Agnes, it's just as easy to ask about two women as it is about one."

"Good thinking. And because we know Irene is dead—in a car crash no less—it probably is a good idea to tell Nash and Steve. I bet they can locate the police report for us."

Jaxson tilted his head. "I have the feeling our former sheriff wasn't the type to store the information electronically."

"No, but the files have to be somewhere."

"Let's hope."

Our food arrived, and I inhaled my muffin. "I wish Nana would show up and tell me why she is really looking for Irene Talbert," I mumbled.

"Glinda?" Rihanna asked.

"Yes?"

"Your necklace is flashing."

I looked down at the pink diamond. Thank goodness it was pulsing pink and not some other color, like yellow, which would imply a person of significant magic was around. On second thought, Nana would qualify since she was a witch.

I checked out the entire restaurant to see if by chance my grandmother had decided to appear even though that wasn't her usual way of contacting me. If she was sufficiently upset over her missing friend—make that her missing dead friend—Nana might show up. No one but me and possibly Rihanna could see her—or so I hoped.

As soon as the warmth and pulsing stopped, I clasped the pendant. "I think Nana was trying to tell me that I need to find out what happened to Irene, despite her having passed. Come to think of it, this might not be about Irene missing as much as the fact her death remains a cold case."

"How do you know it wasn't solved?" Jaxson asked.

"I don't know for sure, but Maude would have said if it had been."

"That's a reasonable assumption, but did you deduce what your grandmother wanted because the stone flashed?" Jaxson asked.

He didn't have to sound so skeptical. "It's a guess. Nana could have been telling me to remind you to find out about Irene's husband."

He chuckled. "The reminder isn't needed. That's my plan."

"Good."

Since a few patrons were waiting for a table, we finished up quickly. After we paid, we headed back to the office. I was excited to find out about Adam Talbert. I tried not to get my hopes up that he'd still be alive, but I was an eternal optimist.

When we entered the office, Iggy was pacing. "What's wrong?" I asked.

"What's wrong? Tippy dive bombed me today."

Tippy was the white seagull with the black-tipped wings who, in theory, was out to get Iggy. Full disclosure: Tippy—or some of his seagull buddies—had left a few reminders on

Iggy's face a month ago, something he'll never forget or forgive.

I didn't bother asking how he knew it was Tippy who'd left the little *reminder*. I wouldn't be surprised to learn that to Iggy, all seagulls were named Tippy.

"You don't look worse for wear." I smiled, hoping to cheer him up.

"Check the handrail. He missed me by an inch."

"Do you want to wear a cap the next time you go outside?" I was kidding, but even if I weren't, I doubt one existed that would fit him. On the other hand, Aunt Fern could make something for Iggy since she'd made several sets of winter clothes for him in the past, not to mention a couple of Halloween costumes.

"No!"

"Why not? At least it would protect your head and eyes."

He faced me. "That would be admitting that Tippy has won this battle."

"I see. I didn't realize you were at war." There was no use arguing with him when he was in this mood.

"We are." His tiny nostrils flared. "Why did you let me come back here in the first place?"

This Tippy thing was getting out of hand. Since Jaxson had been at the office until a little while ago, I had to assume all of this happened after he left. "You asked to come back here. Remember, you don't like Toto, who, by the way, wasn't even there today."

"Figures." Iggy stopped and looked up at me. "Since when do you listen to my demands anyway?"

Ouch. I wasn't in the right frame of mind to deal with his

teenage angst. "We have a clue in our case—assuming you can call trying to find a ghost a case."

"Tell me." Suddenly, Iggy seemed to have forgotten all about his nemesis.

"Jaxson has to do some research, but I'll go over what we've learned so far." I told him Irene's last name, as well as the fact she had a husband who could still be alive. I watered down the information about Wes Armstrong hitting on Nana, but I did mention that Agnes and Nana had a falling out at the end.

Rihanna tapped me on the shoulder. "While you finish up with Iggy, I'm going to speak with Elissa about the two women."

"Perfect. There have to be records on Irene at least."

"I agree, but don't visit her husband without me, okay?"

"Why?" Teenagers usually weren't excited to chat with old people.

She dipped her chin. "So I can tell if he's lying? Mental patients are often kings of manipulation."

I had to think about that. "Pretending to be crazy could be his way to get the State to pay for his room and board."

She smiled. "Now you're catching on." She spun around and left.

I turned to Jaxson. "Should I be insulted that Rihanna thinks some old guy can pull the wool over my eyes?"

Jaxson stepped over to me, placed his hands on my shoulders, and then kissed my forehead. "I'm pleading the fifth."

"You are so funny." I returned my attention back to Iggy. "What do you think?"

"About what?"

Wasn't he listening? "Our plan to find out what happened to Irene." I'm not sure why Iggy would know, but he'd surprised me in the past.

"I hope Steve can help."

"Me, too."

While Jaxson was at his desk researching whether Adam Talbert was still alive, I went into the kitchen to grab some cookies. Since my boyfriend wouldn't want any sweets, being fitness conscience and all, and Rihanna wasn't here, I carried the entire box back to the living room. So what if I'd just polished off a muffin? Stress made me eat.

"I found the number of the Belleview Hospital," Jaxson announced. "I'm going to give them a call to see if an Adam Talbert is a patient."

"Great." I honestly expected the man to have passed, but anything was possible. I hovered over Jaxson as I munched on a cookie.

"Yes. I'm looking for an Adam Talbert." He gave me a thumbs up. "Really? If possible, I'd like to visit him." He listened for a bit. "Oh. Yes, I'm his…grandson." Jaxson looked up at me and shrugged. "Great. We'll be over in a bit." He disconnected and then spun back around to face me. "He's there!"

"Good call on pretending to be a relative."

"They wouldn't have let me see him any other way. Just so you know, Belleview has two wings. Adam Talbert is in the nursing home wing, not the mental ward."

"So much for believing all the gossip." I blew out a breath. "I can't believe Adam Talbert is alive. The fact he is in the nursing home rather than the psyche ward means he's not violent or crazy. That's good. Do we know for sure that he can talk? Not all ninety-year olds are as amazing as Gertrude."

"The receptionist didn't say he couldn't."

"Fantastic. I know that Maude said people think Adam Talbert might have killed his wife, so we have to tread lightly."

"I agree. He should be able to tell us something about the accident, though."

"I hope he remembers it happened." I downed another chocolate chip cookie.

Jaxson pressed the back of his chair against the desk, stretched out his legs, and then crossed his ankles, looking rather relaxed. "If I recall, memories from long ago are the last thing to leave a person, and it's been years since Irene passed."

"I hope you are right."

"Me, too."

Since I'd promised we'd wait from Rihanna, I moved back to the sofa and munched on more chocolate chip cookies until my cousin arrived fifteen minutes later. "Well?" I asked.

She slipped off her purse, plopped down next to me, stuck her hand in the box, and inhaled a cookie. "These are so good."

"They are, aren't they? What did our esteemed medical examiner have to say?"

"Elissa had to look in her files since both women died before her time. Unfortunately, the database isn't the best for old cases. She found nothing on Agnes Lochridge, but she did have something on Irene Talbert."

"That's really good news."

"Yes and no," Rihanna said. "Irene was hit by a car, which we already knew, and she died instantly, but I don't know how that helps us."

"Where did the accident occur?"

"I didn't ask."

"What about the time of day?" I asked.

"Again. I didn't ask."

That wasn't like Rihanna. Usually, she was quite detail-oriented. "That's okay. All of that information should be in the sheriff's report, assuming the accident happened in our town."

"It had to have happened near here, or Irene's case wouldn't be in the system," she said.

"True." I had a smart cousin.

Rihanna looked over at Jaxson. "Did you find anything on Irene's husband?"

"Yes. He's alive, and we are expected in Belleview shortly."

She smiled. "That's great!"

I explained to Iggy that he couldn't come, because Mr. Talbert might freak out.

He lowered his head. "That's okay. I'm good staying here."

Poor Iggy. "Are you good staying because you don't want to go outside, or are you good because you don't want to visit Mr. Talbert?"

"I plead the fifth."

I laughed. He was copying what Jaxson had said. "You can't hide for the rest of your life, you know."

"Maybe Aunt Fern can make me a cape with a hood."

Wasn't he the one who said it would be a sign of weakness if he wore something? "I'll see what she can do."

Hopefully, his foul mood would wear off as soon as we returned with more information.

Once the three of us piled into Jaxson's car, he set the

GPS to the hospital's address, which meant I could relax and not be the map person. I sighed contentedly.

"Do you know what you are going to ask Mr. Talbert?" Jaxson asked once we were on our way.

"Nothing accusatory, though I need to be prepared that he may not even remember his wife."

"Sad but true."

The trip to Belleview was rather scenic, passing one beach town after another. To my surprise, the hospital had a prime location right on the water. I imagine it gave the relatives solace that the patients and inmates—if that was the politically correct name for them—had a nice view.

Once inside, we asked to see Mr. Talbert. Thankfully, the receptionist was so busy talking on her phone to someone she clearly liked that she didn't ask for our identification. Time to go before she remembered the rules about only allowing relatives to visit.

"This is the nursing home wing," I explained to Rihanna. "It's not the mental ward."

"Thanks for letting me know."

When we entered Adam Talbert's room, he appeared to be asleep in his chair. As if he had a sixth sense, he sat up and looked around. "Irene? Is that you?"

Oh, no. Maybe he was living in the past and didn't realize his wife had died.

Jaxson stepped forward. "No, Mr. Talbert. Irene isn't here, but we wanted to talk to you about her."

"Oh. Thank goodness you are all real. You are real, right?"

That implied he might have seen the ghost of his dead wife. "We're real," I answered.

He pointed to a chair in the corner. "Pull that over here.

57

Two of you can sit on the bed."

It was made, so I had no problem doing so. The old man, with his wispy white hair, droopy ears, and scruffy face, seemed nice enough.

I leaner closer to him in case he was hard of hearing. "Can we ask you about Irene's accident?"

His eyes darted right then left. "Accident? Was she hurt?"

Oh, boy. "I'm afraid she was killed, sir, but she didn't suffer."

"She can't be dead. I just saw her." He sounded convincing.

"When?" He might have gotten his years mixed up.

"Maybe a week or so ago. Irene and I broke up many years ago, which was why she only visits me once in a blue moon."

That was really strange, but that gave me an idea. "Did she look the same as always did, or was she kind of transparent?"

He tucked in his chin. "You mean was she a ghost?"

"I suppose."

"No. She was as solid as you are."

If he hadn't seen her ghost, why would he ask if we were real? "Your wife is Irene Talbert, right?"

"Of course she is. And who did you say you were?"

We hadn't said. "My grandmother, Amelia Eagleton, was a good friend of Irene's—as was Agnes Lochridge."

His eyes widened. "I remember them, especially Agnes. Yes, Agnes used to stop by after Irene and I separated."

That was a good start. He did remember. "Now do you remember the hit-and-run accident involving your wife?"

Chapter Six

"HIT-AND-RUN?" MR. TALBERT'S leg bounced, and he wove his fingers together in agitation.

"It happened about six or seven years ago." I wanted to spark his memory—a memory that seemed a bit sporadic at best.

"Oh, yes, I remember now. My wife's car had broken down, and she was walking down the road, hoping to get cell service. That's when someone ran her over."

This was great information, but if he wasn't there, how would he know she was trying to make a call? According to Dr. Sanchez, the report claimed that Irene died immediately. "Did Irene tell you that?"

"Yes, but it was a few years after the accident. No one would let me see her before then. It's how I ended up here."

He wasn't making any sense. Did his wife's death start his mental decline? At first, he didn't know there had been an accident, and then he remembered the details? I could see why he needed to be in a nursing home. I was willing to admit that it was possible he could have learned all of this from the police report.

His head lolled to the side, and his eyes closed. Had he really just fallen asleep? "Mr. Talbert?"

When he didn't rouse, Rihanna stepped over to him and tapped him on the shoulder. "Sir? Are you okay?"

He jerked awake and looked around. "Irene?"

"No, Mr. Talbert. I'm Rihanna."

Oh, boy. Clearly, asking further questions would get us nowhere.

"If I leave you my business card, can you call me if you see your wife again? Or better yet, can you tell her to call me?"

"Yes, I will."

Before we left, we asked him if he needed anything, but he said the staff took care of his every need. I was certain there was a lot more to the story, but for now, we'd probably overstayed our visit.

I couldn't wait to hear what Jaxson and Rihanna thought of this man. On our way out, we passed several people in wheelchairs staring off into space, and it saddened me. Right now, though, I needed to focus on Adam Talbert.

Once in the car, I asked Jaxson and Rihanna their opinions on the mental stability of Irene's husband.

"He wasn't telling the truth," Rihanna said.

"I had that same impression. Which part was a lie?"

"When he said he didn't know Irene had died. The strange part was after he dropped the ruse of not remembering, he believed it when he said that she visited him every once in a while."

"We are talking ghosts here, right?" I had no other explanation.

"That's my take," she said.

As Jaxson pulled onto the main road and headed back to Witch's Cove, he told us his thoughts. "He could be hallucinating since he doesn't seem to have accepted his wife's death. It could be why he said she visited him. He wanted it to be true so badly that he imagined her."

"That certainly could be the case. Something else he said made no sense. How come he wasn't allowed to see her? Could he have been referring to her body in the morgue?" I asked.

"Most likely," Jaxson said.

"If you were his actual grandson, then you could have spoken with his doctor to find out his real mental state."

"True, but I'm not. Don't worry, we'll figure something out," Jaxson said.

We didn't say much more on the trip back home. I, for one, was trying to process what we'd learned. When we finally arrived in Witch's Cove, a wave of fatigue hit me. "Guys, I'm kind of beat. How about we wait until tomorrow to stop at the sheriff's office to ask about Irene's hit-and-run? If we can get a look at the accident report, things might become clearer."

"Fine by me," Jaxson said.

"Me, too," Rihanna added. "I want to give Gavin a call anyway."

That was sweet. "I hope Sheriff Duncan's report will give us a clue as to why someone might have run her over," I said.

"Once you know that, then what?" he asked.

"I don't know, but the next time the ghosts show up, I'll be more prepared with questions."

He smiled. "Sounds like a plan."

"I'd like to join you tomorrow, if it's okay?" Rihanna asked.

"Absolutely." My cousin often picked up on clues that I missed.

After a quick kiss goodnight, Jaxson took off. I entered the apartment, only to be met with a million questions from Iggy. "I have answers, but let me get some tea, and we'll discuss it."

THE NEXT MORNING, I was rudely awoken by my alarm. We had work to do, and we wouldn't solve this case if I slept in too late, which was all I wanted to do. As soon as I dressed, Iggy and I headed over to the office. No surprise, he kept hidden in my purse, not once popping up to ask any other questions about Irene. I had to conclude that Tippy must have been on his mind.

When I walked in, both Rihanna and Jaxson looked ready to go and check out Irene's accident report. I set down my purse to allow Iggy to crawl out. "You good to stay here?" I asked him.

"I'm good, but if I'm gone when you get back, it means I'm on patrol."

"Patrol?"

"Last night, I had a lot of time to think about that flying menace. I need to know when and where the seagulls go every hour of the day. It's the only way to be prepared for their next attack."

Attack? Ugh. I supposed if it would keep him busy, I was game. "Sounds like a good strategy. I'm glad you're taking things into your own hands and not letting that nasty seagull intimidate you."

"You got that right."

His overconfidence, however, could get him into trouble. It's not as if Iggy possessed many defenses against a seagull. "Just be careful out there, and be sure to keep an eye on the sky."

"Roger that." Iggy was clearly watching too much television.

The three of us walked across the street to the sheriff's office. When we entered, Pearl was at her desk knitting, implying it was a slow morning.

She put down her needles. "Come to report a crime?"

That seemed to be her new opening line. I guess people never showed up just to chat. "No, or did something happen that we should be aware of?"

Pearl waved hand. "I wish. It's just your typical slow day in Witch's Cove. How can I help you?"

"Is Steve here?"

"No, but Nash is."

Since neither had been in town six years ago, I supposed it didn't really matter which officer we spoke with. "He'll do."

She nodded that we could go on back. Clearly, our town wasn't big on formalities.

Nash was at his desk pouring over something on his computer. When he heard us, he looked up. "This is a surprise."

Why did everyone keep saying that? We often were there to deal with some tragedy or another. "We'd like to see what you have on an old cold case."

"How old?"

"Maybe six years?"

"You want to come into the conference room and tell me what this is about?" He didn't really have a lot of room for all of us to sit near him. That, or he thought it would be best to keep our conversation out of Pearl's earshot.

"Sure."

We followed Nash into the room and sat down. "Tell me what this is about. Or does this have to do with the other night's *sighting* at the beach."

"Hunter told you?" I shouldn't have been surprised. Those two went way back.

"Seeing ghosts can be quite a shock to the system. He wanted a reality check."

"I can understand that. In retrospect, I should have prepared him better."

"I'm not sure anyone can be prepared for something like that."

"Is he okay?" I hoped Hunter wasn't too upset.

"He is, but he wouldn't say much more. What's going on?"

Even though Nash wasn't a warlock, he understood the occult. Since he was a werewolf, out-of-the-box ideas were the norm for him. I explained that one of the ghosts referenced a woman by the name of Irene. "She also said that my grandmother was worried about her since she was missing."

"That led you to conclude what exactly?"

I detailed our findings about this woman who we later learned was Irene Talbert. "She was a victim of a hit-and-run accident about six years ago. Rihanna spoke with Elissa who was able to find her autopsy report. Elissa confirmed that Irene had indeed been run over. What we'd like to know is whether there is any information on file as to whether the driver was ever found and charged."

"We have files, but the problem is that they are in the back room in boxes. Apparently, the former sheriff wasn't a big fan of organization or digitization."

Sheriff Duncan's disregard for protocol and modernization might be why he was rotting away in jail right now. "Can we take a look?"

Nash seemed to be working hard to suppress a smile. "Be my guest. I hope you aren't allergic to dust?"

"That bad, huh?"

"Yup. Come with me." He pushed back his chair, and we followed him down a hallway to a back room that I never knew existed.

Nash was right. The inside was a nightmare. Piled high from floor to ceiling were boxes, many of which were covered in dust. I sneezed three times. "Sorry. Is there any order to this?"

"Order?" Nash laughed. "Seriously, there could be, but Steve and I haven't seen the need to go through this mess. These are old cases. There is a ladder against the wall if you want to get the ones down from the top, but I need to be in here when you look through them."

"Great. So you'll help?"

He chuckled. "Before I commit, let me see if I'm understanding this. You want to forage through all of these boxes for a six-year old case in order to help your grandmother, a grandmother who has passed, right?"

"Yes. I don't want to spend my life worrying that a bunch of ghosts are going to haunt me if I ignore them. They're the ones who want me to find out about Irene. I'm sure of it."

I didn't think that Agnes, Gladys, Wes, or Neil would ever haunt me, but I needed some explanation. Actually, my need to do this stemmed from my unending curiosity, as well as my desire to help Nana.

"Okay then. Let's get started."

First order of business was to find some logic to this pile of boxes. Jaxson was the tallest, so he was better suited to check out the ones near the top. "Can you see the dates on those boxes up there?" I asked him.

After dusting off many of the fronts in order to read the printed dates, he studied them. "It appears as if the oldest cases are against this far wall. The sheriff started at the bottom and added boxes as he went."

I turned to Nash. "These are just the files, right? The evidence is someplace else, I presume?" I didn't need to see anything gruesome this early in the day.

He chuckled. "Absolutely. We have an evidence locker, which is secure. These are merely the case reports. If we ever hire an apprentice, we might ask him or her to digitize it all."

"That would take a lifetime."

"You might be right."

After we checked the dates on the boxes, we found eight that fit the time frame. The four of us then split the daunting task of locating Irene's file.

"Can we sit in the conference room and look through these? There's not a lot of space in here." Not only that, my eyes were starting to water from the dust.

"Sure. I'll ask Pearl to get us some coffee and snacks."

"You are the best, Deputy Solano."

He smiled. "I bet you won't think so after a few hours of looking through these files. It will be a boring task."

I didn't think it would take that long to find Irene Talbert's name. "We'll see."

Jaxson handed us two boxes each that we carried into the conference room. Turns out, I was right. In less than thirty minutes, Rihanna hit pay dirt.

"I got it." She smiled and waved the folder.

"Let me see it." Nash lifted his chin. "After all, I'm trained to interpret these things." He then shot us a grin.

Nash opened the folder and took his time pouring over it. To be fair, the folder was rather thick.

When he finished, he looked up. "Okay. This is what I've gleaned from my quick perusal. Irene Talbert was found about a hundred yards from her car with her cell phone in her hand. Apparently, she wasn't able to get a signal, but the last number she dialed belonged to her husband. I won't go into the gory details, but she was hit from behind. The impact killed her instantly."

"Were there any skid marks?" Jaxson asked.

Nash looked through the pages again. "No."

"What time of day was it?" A daytime accident would make it more likely to have been murder.

Nash consulted the folder again. "The medical examiner put the time of death around ten at night."

So much for that theory. "Is it possible the person didn't see Irene?" I asked.

"Anything is possible, but the driver would have known he or she had hit something. The report doesn't mention any signs of tire tracks on the side of the road to indicate that the

VELLA DAY

person had stopped. Not only that, the driver didn't call 9-1-1."

Then it was a definite hit-and-run. "How long before she was found?"

He scanned the details again. "The next morning. A passing motorist spotted her.

"That is so sad."

"Any suspects?" Rihanna asked.

Nash swallowed a smile. "The sheriff questioned the very distraught husband, but he claimed he had an alibi. Adam Talbert was in bed long before ten. Considering his age at the time, he was probably telling the truth, but we'll never know."

Alibis could be faked. I wouldn't be surprised to find out that Sheriff Duncan didn't do a lot of follow up despite the thickness of the folder.

"Did the husband suggest any suspects?" I asked.

"One person."

"Who?" I shouldn't have to ask.

"An Agnes Lochridge."

"No way."

"Just because she has passed doesn't mean she didn't commit murder when she was alive. You said you'd never met her," Nash said.

He was right, but I didn't want it to be true. "No, but she was one of the ghosts, and she seemed nice. Actually, Agnes sounded like a caring person."

His brows rose. "And what did she have to say about Irene's death?"

I had to think if she said anything. "Nothing. She only told us that my grandmother was upset that Irene was missing.

She never hinted that Irene was dead."

"Then why say she was missing if she'd already passed? There wasn't a mention of a grave robbery."

I pointed a finger at him. "That is the question of the day. I'm getting the idea that this magical afterlife isn't what we've been taught to believe."

He leaned forward. "How so?"

Since Nash was a werewolf, maybe he believed he'd go to a special place when he died. "I don't know, but I plan to find out." Nash nodded.

"Did the report say if they questioned Agnes?" Jaxson asked.

"The sheriff spoke with her, but she said she hadn't been driving that night—or any night. Her eyesight was too bad to go out when it was dark."

"That might be true. I remember Nana complaining of the same issue."

Nash leaned back in his chair. "What is your next move?"

"I'm not sure. We spoke with Irene's husband, but he is in a nursing home and seems a bit confused. He never mentioned that Agnes might have been guilty, only that he knew her."

The deputy dipped his chin. "You were going to mention this visit when?"

"Sorry. I was a little distracted."

"When you do find out something, please let us know. This is a cold case, but if the husband is still alive, he deserves closure."

"Assuming he wasn't the one who ran her over," I mumbled.

Nash looked over the file again. "It says here, he and Irene had recently separated, which was why Adam was unaware of her whereabouts on the night of the hit-and-run."

"I didn't know there had been trouble in paradise. That being said, people lie. Thank you for letting us look through these files."

"You bet. Anytime."

"Let's help Nash put these boxes back," I announced with as much joy as I could muster.

Once we'd put everything away, we left the office. I suggested a coffee, since either Pearl forgot to bring us some, or Nash hadn't asked her.

"Do you think Miriam will be able to add to this story?" Jaxson asked.

"Her sister knew about the hit-and-run. It's possible Miriam knows more."

He smiled and wrapped an arm around my shoulder. "I say we ask her."

Chapter Seven

J AXSON HELD OPEN the door to the Bubbling Cauldron Coffee shop. As soon as Rihanna and I entered, the rich aroma of coffee beans had me yearning for some strong brew. When I spotted Miriam at the counter, I waved.

No sooner had we found our seat when she came over. "I heard you've been busy."

I had to assume either her sister had called her or Pearl had. After all, I had asked Pearl to do some reconnaissance for us. "We have been. You have a minute?"

"For gossip?" I nodded, and she grinned. "Always."

"I guess you know that we're looking into the death or maybe murder of Irene Talbert. In case you didn't know, Irene was a friend of my grandmother's."

"I did know, but why bring this up after all these years?"

"Jaxson and I are free at the moment, and this cold case intrigues me." I hope she bought that. Eventually, everyone would learn of my ghost sightings, especially since so many had seen them. For now, though, I wanted to keep it simple. Fingers crossed that Pearl hadn't blabbed about it yet.

"How can I help?" Miriam asked.

"Did you know Irene?" I asked.

"A long time ago we were in a book club together."

I liked that. "Do you have any idea who might have killed her?"

"No. We weren't close. I know everyone thought her husband might have run her over, but I didn't see any motive."

"What do you mean?" I asked.

"Irene told me that she found out that Adam was having an affair. And no, I never learned who this woman was. I know people said they thought Adam was guilty, but he had no reason to kill his wife." She hesitated. "Though with Irene dead, Adam wouldn't have to pay alimony, but that seems far-fetched to me. I could almost believe the other way around. Irene might have had motive to kill him. Besides, Irene had already moved out of their house by the time she was killed."

Miriam learned all of this from attending a book club? Wow. Maybe I should start one. My mind jumped to another possibility. Could Agnes have been this mystery woman? If the authorities had found out the mistress' identity, the information should be in the file. "I assume Irene was rather upset about the existence of this other woman?" I know that might sound like a dumb question, but she could have been happy, especially if Adam was the weak man others portrayed him to be.

"Are you kidding? She was totally devastated."

I had misjudged her then. "Oh."

"I think she only came to the book club because she needed to be around people. Her depression was quite severe."

"Are you saying she was suicidal?" I had a minor in psychology, but a little bit of knowledge could be dangerous.

Miriam shrugged. "I couldn't say for sure. She never

mentioned wanting to harm herself, but often we don't know until after the person takes their own life."

"Remember, ladies, that someone ran her over," Jaxson said. "She didn't jump off a bridge or anything."

"I know, but maybe the easiest way to end her life was to hire someone to do it for her." That was a horrible thought. "I should ask if there was any evidence to indicate Irene had been that desperate—like did she send any messages to an unknown person or make a clandestine payment?"

Miriam shook her head. "I wouldn't know anything about that, but it would be in the police report if they uncovered anything. All I can say for sure is that the women in the book club were so upset over Irene's death that we disbanded the group. That meant the line of gossip dried up."

Why didn't I believe that? Gossip never stopped flowing in Witch's Cove. "Who else was in the group?"

Miriam glanced to the ceiling. "Gosh, it's been so many years, and many of the women came and went, I can't recall."

Rihanna would know if she was lying, unless Miriam was able to block her thoughts somehow. Mental stress often did that. "If you think of any names, let me know."

She smiled. "I will. Now, what can I get you all?"

That sounded like a dodge to me, but I didn't pressure her. Instead, we ordered, and she left to prepare our drinks.

I looked over at Rihanna to see if what Miriam said was the whole truth and nothing but the truth. "Your thoughts?"

"She's keeping something from us. I'm suspecting she knows who was in the group, but maybe she doesn't want us to bug them."

"I don't blame her. She's probably trying to protect them

from having to relive the tragedy. Thanks."

"Do you really think Irene was suicidal?" Jaxson asked.

"She could have been. Maybe that's why Nana is worried about her, though what more could Irene do now that she's already dead?"

He planted his elbows on the table. "Do you think that people carry their emotional baggage with them once they die?"

Was that possible? "That doesn't sound right, but maybe they do. Look at our last case where the ghosts returned to torment their killer. They wanted revenge—and got it."

Jaxson seemed to think about that. "I guess you're right."

"If Irene is missing," Rihanna said, "could she have returned to Witch's Cove because she wanted to find out who killed her?"

"That sounds reasonable, but that means she'd have to be away from witch Nirvana for quite some time."

"Witch Nirvana?" Jaxson asked.

"I needed a name, and I didn't think it was appropriate to call it Heaven since that is where regular humans go." The thought of not being reunited with Jaxson after we both passed made my stomach churn. I hope I was wrong about the afterlife being divided.

"Gotcha. Witch Nirvana. That sounds nice."

I thought so, too. I looked between Jaxson and Rihanna. "How would you two describe Irene to someone. You both must have an image in your head."

Rihanna glanced upward before returning her focus to us. "If she were alive today, I'd say she was an angry and depressed person."

"I certainly would believe the angry part, and I can't blame her for that if her husband took up with another woman." I touched Jaxson's hand. "If I found out you wanted someone else, I'd be devastated."

"You have nothing to worry about, pink lady. There's only one woman in my life."

"Aw. Thank you." Happy, I continued. "Tell me your impression of Irene."

"She's a take charge woman. Because her husband cheated on her, she left him. I respect that." Jaxson leaned back in his chair, seemingly pleased with his assessment.

These two had completely different opinions of Irene. "You don't think she took her own life then?" That was assuming Miriam was accurate in her assessment.

"No. Never," he said.

"Okay. We should see if someone knows where Adam and Irene used to live. Some of their neighbors might still be there and would be willing to tell us more. If those two had an altercation, or if there was another woman, I'm betting the neighbors would know."

Jaxson smiled. "I knew there was a reason why I went into business with you."

He was the sweetest man alive. Just then Miriam delivered our food. "By any chance, do you know where the Talberts used to live?" I asked her.

"Sure. They lived south of here in the Wildwood subdivision. I couldn't tell you the house number, but I think Christina Thompson sold the house after Adam was put in a home. She'd know."

"Thanks. We'll check with her. Oh. I forgot to ask if the

Talberts had any children?" If so, they might have an idea what might have happened to their mom.

Miriam pressed her lips together. "Not that I know of."

"Oh, well. It was worth asking." I picked up my coffee that probably contained more milk than java, blew across the top to cool it a bit, and then sipped on it. "Yum. Delicious as always."

Miriam smiled and then headed back to the counter.

"I take it our next stop is Thompson Realty?" Jaxson asked.

"It can't hurt."

"What if I give them a call instead? That will save us a trip."

"Great." I might have been the math major, but Jaxson's ability to find efficient methods surpassed anything I could do.

"I'll need to step outside though." He nodded to the rather noisy table near us.

"Gotcha."

Once Jaxson left, Rihanna faced me. "It's not even noon. Do you think the neighbors will be home?"

"The elderly ones would be. I'm just hoping those who were close to the Talberts are still alive."

"True."

About a minute later, Jaxson returned, waved his phone, and sat down. "I got a hold of Christina She is investigating the address and will get back to us."

"Awesome." It almost felt as if we had a good shot at figuring out this case. "I wonder if Duncan Donuts ever spoke to the neighbors?" That was my nickname for the portly

Sheriff Duncan.

"If he did, it would be in the file back at the station."

"Do you think Nash would consider making a copy of the file for us?" I asked.

"You can ask him. The worst he can say is no," Jaxson said.

"I bet it's illegal to share that information about a case, but I don't know for sure," Rihanna said.

"It's a cold case. What does he have to lose? He knows we'll let him take the win on the arrest, though it's possible whoever ran over Irene is dead."

Jaxson shook his head. "Irene only died about six years ago. While there are a lot of eighty-something-year olds driving, not many go out at night. Think about what that means."

It took me a second to put the pieces together. "Due to poor eyesight, you think our killer is younger?" That would narrow the suspect list.

He shrugged. "Maybe."

"It's a good theory. When I set up my whiteboard to list our suspects, I'll add a column for age."

He smiled and then sipped his coffee. A slight moan escaped and then his shoulders relaxed. "That is good."

I loved seeing him happy. "Miriam makes the best."

Jaxson's phone rang a few minutes later, and he picked up his phone. "Jaxson Harrison." He motioned for something to write with. Who carried a pen and paper anymore? All I had was my phone.

"Forty-seven Mayville Lane?" He nodded toward my note app that I'd pulled up on my phone, and I quickly typed it in.

"Thanks, Christina. We owe you." He disconnected.

When we finished our drink and snack, I turned to Rihanna. "Do you want to come with us?" I needed our lie detector.

"Absolutely. I'm always up for an adventure."

Jaxson paid and we headed to his car. Finding Mayville Lane was a bit of a challenge, but we finally made it after taking two wrong turns. For future reference, the GPS is not infallible.

The home Adam Talbert used to live in wasn't what I expected. I whistled. "That is a mansion."

"Did you learn what he did for a living?" Jaxson asked.

"No, but he must have been rich to afford a place like this."

"Look," Rihanna said. "A woman is sitting on her porch swing next door."

"That's perfect." This woman's home was an eyesore compared to Adam Talbert's former home. In fact, his place was the nicest on the street. "I wonder if the new owners fixed up the place, or if this was what it looked like when they purchased it."

"Why would that matter?" Jaxson asked.

"I don't know, but it might mean something."

Jaxson smiled, cut the engine, and pushed open his door. Rihanna and I followed him out.

"What are you going to ask her?" Rihanna said as we walked down the driveway.

"I'll start with seeing how well she knew either Irene or Adam Talbert."

"Sounds good."

I didn't like descending on the poor woman like this, but it wasn't like we had a choice. I nudged Jaxson. "Why don't you start the conversation."

"Why me?"

"You're good with women."

He chuckled and wrapped an arm around my waist. "Come on."

The elderly woman in the blue flowered dress kept her gaze on us as we approached, appearing more curious than scared, though I didn't think we looked particularly intimidating.

"Hello, ma'am." Jaxson smiled and stopped a good six-feet from her.

She adjusted her tortoise shell eyeglasses and then did a quick scan of Jaxson. "I don't got no money, so if you're askin', you ain't gettin' any."

Jaxson pulled out his wallet and whipped out a ten dollar bill. Really? We never bribed people, though this might have been more charity than anything.

"We've come to pay for a bit of gossip."

She smiled. "Come sit down, young man."

Jaxson held out the money, but she shook her head. "Don't feel right taking something that I'm willing to give freely. Instead, take these two young ladies out to dinner."

I didn't tell her that ten dollars wouldn't go as far today as it did in the past. We dragged over some chairs and faced her. "Did you know the Talberts?" I asked.

"Oh, I sure did. Such a shame about Irene. I heard it was quick though."

She must be talking about the hit-and-run. "It was."

"Any idea who had it out for her?" Jaxson asked.

"Got a lot of suspects, but my main one is that floozie Adam took up with." She glanced over at the house. "Many say it's why Irene left."

The fact she didn't know for sure implied she and Irene weren't the best of buds.

My pulse soared. "Do you know this woman's name?" Please don't say it was Agnes.

"I'm kind of hard of hearing, so I can't be a hundred percent sure, but it might have been a woman named Sal."

Sal? "Did you hear Adam call her that?"

"Sure did."

"How old was she?" Rihanna asked.

The older woman shifted her gaze to my cousin. "Not young like you, but not too old either. She looked closer to fifty, but ten bucks says she had a lot of work done and was really over sixty."

That would make the two of them having about a twenty-five-year age difference. If Adam had money, he probably thought he could buy some arm candy.

"Can you describe her?" Though the chances of finding this woman would be slim.

This woman leaned forward. "Between you and me, she looked like a hooker."

Hence the floozy comment. "Can you be more specific?"

"Well, she wore them super high heels, so it was hard to tell her height, but she had platinum blonde hair. Kind of looked like an older version of Marilyn Monroe." Her cheer suddenly disappeared. "Do you youngsters even know who that is?"

Rihanna held up her hand. "Everyone knows of the legend."

Our gossip queen leaned back against her swing, seemingly happy. "I'm glad to hear it."

I tried to figure out what else I needed to know. "What is your name?"

"Jean Elkhart."

"Nice to meet you, Ms. Elkhart." I introduced us in case we needed to contact her again.

"When did Irene move out of the house?" Jaxson asked.

"I can't recall exactly," Jean said. "It might have been a month before Sal started coming around more frequently."

"Do you have any idea what happened to Sal?" I asked.

She shook her head. "No, I'm sorry."

"Are there any other neighbors who were good friends with either Irene or Adam?" Not that Jean hadn't been helpful, but it was always good to get a different perspective.

"Everyone who used to live here back then has either moved away or is dead. It's sad, really."

I felt sorry for her. I held out my card to her, but she motioned I place it on the table. "If you think of anything, give me a call?"

She smiled. "I'd like that."

In silence, we headed back to the car. Even though we believed we knew the reason for the break-up between Irene and Adam, it would be very helpful if we could find Sal and speak to her. It was always possible she was the hit-and-run driver, especially if she thought Adam was planning to get back with his wife.

We piled into the car. "Any idea how we can find this

woman?" I asked.

"If she was as put together as Ms. Elkhart claims, I bet Priscilla knows her," Rihanna suggested.

Pricilla was the owner of a high-end nail and spa in town. I turned around in the seat. "You are one smart girl."

She grinned. "Why, thank you."

Jaxson looked over at me. "I assume you will be checking out Moon Bay Nail Spa next?"

"It's the best lead we've had so far."

Chapter Eight

AFTER I CHECKED in with my familiar to make sure he and Tippy hadn't had any further altercations, I walked down the street to Priscilla DeLorean's place. There was only a fifty-fifty chance the owner would be there, and even if she was, Priscilla could be with a client. Since I didn't have any other clues to follow at the moment, I was willing to wait.

To my delight, Priscilla was there and said she could take me as soon as she finished with her current customer. Twenty minutes later, I was escorted to her station.

Her eyes widened. "Well, well. How long has it been, Glinda?"

"Too long."

Priscilla lifted my hands and shook her head. "At least I can't be jealous that you went to another salon."

I did my own nails now, but they lacked the professional skill Priscilla always provided. "I'm here now!"

"Great, pick out your color and then have a seat."

I could have just asked about Sal and left, but I liked to pay for my information. Choosing a color usually was easy since I always went with pink, but this time, I was in the mood for something darker. "What do you think of this red?"

Her brows rose. "What's the occasion?"

I've been communicating with ghosts. "No reason. Every once in a while I like a change."

"Change is good, but how about a dark plum? Red is too common for you."

I liked that idea. I chose a different polish and handed it to Priscilla. She sat across from me and started by removing my old, chipped polish. "By any chance, do you have a client by the name of Sal?" Pricilla did more than nails. Waxing, facials, and massages were but a few of her services—as was gossip.

"You have a case, don't you?" She sounded excited.

"Yes. I'm hoping this woman can help with our murder investigation. Sal—no last name—has platinum blonde hair, loves to wear high heels, and is very high maintenance."

Priscilla sobered. "That sounds like Sally Gentran, or should I say that was Sally Gentran."

"She's dead?" Please say no. I needed this woman for information.

"Murdered."

"Oh, no. When did this happen?"

"I'd say maybe five or six years ago."

The timing wasn't lost on me. I'd just graduated from college and was teaching out of town at the time, which was why I was unaware of all this tragedy. "That must have been quite a time for gossip. First Irene Talbert and then Sally Gentran."

"It was."

That implied she knew about Irene's death. Good. I waited for her to say more, but she didn't, possibly because Priscilla might have thought I already knew about the relationship between Sally and Adam Talbert. "Did they ever find out who killed Sally?"

"Nah. All I heard was that she was poisoned."

Poison often implied a female killer. Witches, especially, liked that method of death, and I'm talking about the bad witches here. We good ones would never harm anyone. "I heard Sally and Adam Talbert were tight."

Her eyes widened. "You knew about that? Sally was very careful to keep that on the down low."

She didn't totally keep her mouth shut if she told Priscilla. "I heard it from Adam's neighbor."

Priscilla finished removing my polish and then began the challenging task of taming my cuticles. "Is that so?"

"Yes. Do you know if Irene knew about Sally?"

"My lips are sealed."

I hated it when people didn't want to gossip. "But Sally is dead—as is Irene. Don't you want to find out what happened to them? Sally's family must want some closure, too."

Priscilla leaned back and let out a long breath. "You're right."

"Thank you. Does Sally have any family?"

"Not in Witch's Cove, I don't think, but to be honest, we didn't chat much about them. She was just so happy that Adam was always lavishing her with gifts, it was all she talked about."

That made sense. "Did she mention Irene, Adam's wife?"

Priscilla looked off to the side. "Not often. No one likes to be the *other woman*, but Sally said their marriage was on the rocks before she entered the scene."

That wasn't what I'd heard, but who knew the real truth

besides Irene and Adam? They might have had trouble before, and Sally was the catalyst that caused Irene to leave.

If I questioned Adam again, I doubt he would be honest about it—assuming he even remembered what happened.

Priscilla applied the base coat and then placed my fingers in the nail dryer. I couldn't help but wonder how many more cold cases existed under Sheriff Duncan's reign.

I wish I could let this go, but I couldn't, not when I had a good source here. "Do you know who was friends with Sally?"

"This may sound terrible, but when Sally would start talking, I would drift off. I know that makes me look bad, but she repeated the same thing over and over again. It was Adam bought me this today, or Adam bought me that." She smiled. "Sally was nothing like you, Glinda. You always come with something interesting to talk about."

I doubted that, but it was nice of her to say. It didn't take her long to finish the color and top coat. When I believed I'd sufficiently picked her brain, I paid and left with the promise not to wait so long in between visits.

On the walk back, I kept looking at my nails, really liking how nice they were for a change. Jaxson never criticized my appearance, but I should do more for myself.

When I reached the staircase to the office, I checked on the hibiscus plant. It needed some water and a good cleaning from the salt, the dust, and the bird droppings. A few of the leaves were half eaten, and I hoped Iggy had been the one to munch on them and not the seagulls. If not, my familiar might be right about Tippy and his friends having it out for him.

To my surprise, when I arrived, Penny was in the office.

She swung around. "There you are. How did it go? Jaxson said you were working on a lead."

"I was." I hugged Penny. "Gather around people, and I will tell you what I found out."

Jaxson swung his chair around, and Rihanna moved over to the seat across from the sofa so I could sit next to Penny. "The bad news is that Sal—aka Sally Gentran—is dead."

Rihanna sighed. "I was really hoping she could give us some idea who might have killed Irene."

"Me, too." I relayed everything Priscilla told me about Sally, including some of the inconsistencies.

"Did Priscilla give you any ideas where to look next?" Jaxson asked.

"No. She didn't think Sally had any family in town, but even if she did, I bet Sally wouldn't have told them much more than some guy was lavishing gifts on her." I turned to Penny. "What did you find out about Agnes Lochridge?"

"A fair amount, actually. I spoke to two women who were friends with Agnes, both of whom are in nursing homes. I also talked with one former neighbor."

"I'm impressed!" I said.

Penny grinned. "Thanks. It's been an interesting day. So these two nursing home women loved Agnes. They said she was kind and always wanted to help others. Turns out, Agnes and her husband, Herb, had been good friends with Irene and Adam for years."

That was news. "I was aware that Agnes, Irene, and Nana were friends but not that the Lochridges and the Talberts were close."

"There's more. After Agnes' husband died, she and your

grandmother became inseparable, and Agnes still remained fond of the Talberts."

Jaxson rested his elbows on his knees and dangled his fingers between his legs. "Don't tell me that after Irene and Adam split that Agnes saw her chance to move in on Adam?"

She smiled. "It's possible, but I don't think so. Being the nice person that she was, Agnes visited Adam to be his sounding board, nothing more.

"So she claimed." All right, I couldn't help myself.

"I don't think she was there to seduce him. Apparently, after Irene left him, Adam was so guilt ridden at having the affair that he unburdened his soul to Agnes."

Was that all? Something wasn't connecting for me. "If that was true, why did Nana and Agnes go their separate ways? And why did he continue to see Sally and give her gifts if he was torn up about his wife?"

Penny held up a finger. "That is where it gets juicy. The details from the former neighbor were a little vague, but she told me that Agnes was arrested for stalking someone."

I never would have guessed that. That might have precipitated the change in her relationship with Nana. "Who did she stalk?"

"Your woman, Sally Gentran."

I whistled. "Did this person say why?"

"She didn't want to speculate."

"Maybe she didn't want to say anything bad about her friend, Agnes," Rihanna added.

Penny shrugged. "That might be true."

"Just guessing here," Jaxson said, "but if Agnes was friends with Irene, maybe she was spying for her to see how often

Sally and the husband were together."

"I would totally do that for a friend," Penny said.

"Me, too." I snapped my fingers. "I think a trip back to the sheriff's office might be in order."

Jaxson looked upward. "Don't tell me you want to find the file that indicates Agnes was arrested, because you think it might state the reason for the stalking?"

He knew me so well. "Maybe. Not that I don't believe Penny's source, but yes, Agnes' statement might be included as to why she was following Sally, though it's always possible Agnes would have lied about it."

"If Irene asked Agnes to spy for her, it implies Irene still felt something for Adam," he said.

"True." I turned to Rihanna. "I hate to ask, but do you think you could see what the autopsy report said about Sally Gentran. I'd like to know if the cause of death was poison."

"Sure, but if you're thinking that some magical potion was involved, I doubt there will be any mention of it."

"I know, but there might be something in the report that is useful." I turned to Jaxson. "In the meantime, how about if we bug Nash again. I'm curious what the report will say."

He crossed his arms. "Are you sure you want to go down this rabbit hole?"

"What do you mean?"

"If you investigate how or why Agnes died, how Sally died, and how everyone else connected to the case died, we could be looking into every cold case for the last few years. Don't forget how many boxes there are in the back room."

Why did he always have to bring me down to Earth? "You don't think it matters what the reports say?"

"Not really. You said Sally was poisoned. Whether that is true or not, bottom line is that she is dead. That's important."

"I know, but Sheriff Duncan must have interviewed Agnes if people suspected her."

He nodded. "True, but are you thinking she harmed Sally? Sure, she stalked her, but would she go so far as to poison her?"

I slumped back against the sofa. "She is a witch, or at least I think she is. She'd be able to do it."

"Being capable of murder, and doing it, are two very different things," he said.

"I get it."

"For the sake of argument, let's suppose Agnes did kill Sally, how does that help us find Irene, let alone identify Irene's killer?"

Jaxson was right. To be honest, Jaxson was usually right. "Okay. You win."

"It's not about winning, Glinda. It's about planning the best use of our time. I agree that the living Agnes might have played a role in Irene's disappearance somehow, but until we know more, we shouldn't accuse her."

I didn't think it mattered since Agnes was already dead. It wasn't as if she'd go to jail. "I wish I could talk to Nana. She could clear up a few things."

Rihanna twisted toward me. "Here's a thought. Do you think Agnes would be in the same place as Nana if she were a killer? Or be concerned that Nana was upset regarding Irene being missing if she'd killed Irene?"

"I hadn't even considered that, but I hope not. Who knows what the justice system is like up there?" I was driving myself crazy and probably should focus on the facts.

"Why don't I drag out the white board?" Jaxson suggested. "That way, you can do your own magic on it."

"That's a good idea. It often helps unscramble my mind when I write things down."

Jaxson stood, went into the back, and returned with the white board. I debated asking Drake and Andorra to stop over, but it wouldn't hurt to do a trial run with Jaxson, Rihanna, Penny, and Iggy. I looked for my familiar but didn't see him, though I was sure he was hiding somewhere.

"Where are you Iggy?" I called to him.

"I think he went out a bit ago," Rihanna said.

"Darn. I hope he doesn't pick a fight with Tippy. I know who would lose that battle." My familiar would.

"He can take care of himself." Jaxson always came to his defense.

"Physically, yes, but what about emotionally?"

Jaxson dipped his chin. "Seriously? Sometimes you need to let the kid figure things out for himself."

I didn't want to get into an argument over Iggy. If we ever married and had kids, I had to learn to listen to reason. "Okay."

As if Iggy had been waiting to make his grand entrance, he flew through the cat door, his tail whipping back and forth. "Quick. Grab your camera."

Rihanna jerked to attention at the word *camera*. "Why?"

"Tippy is out there eating my hibiscus. Can't you hear him screaming, or squawking, or whatever that annoying sound is called?"

I had read up on seagulls and their habits. "He's screaming to make you afraid. He doesn't want you bothering him."

"Me? Bothering him? He's eating *my* plant."

Jaxson stood and pulled out his cell phone from his pocket. "I'll see what I can do."

"Be careful," Iggy said. "If Tippy knows you're with me, he might dive bomb you."

I could tell Jaxson was trying not to laugh. He bent down and swooped up Iggy. "Me be careful? That's not how this works, buddy. You can't make others fight your fight. We'll do this together. Got it?"

"Yes, sir."

Yes, sir? I'd never heard Iggy be compliant in his life. It must be Jaxson's take charge attitude that did it. As soon as Jaxson opened the door, the screeching from the gull blew in. I had to admit, the sound was intense and rather unpleasant.

"Good luck," I called after them. I shook my head. "I wonder what benefit photographing the crime scene would do. Even if Jaxson captured half the seagull population chomping on the plant, it's not like he could have them arrested."

Rihanna laughed. "So true. What are we going to do with Iggy?"

"I guess part of growing up is learning to deal with bullies. Right now, I have to figure out what to do about Irene."

Chapter Nine

"ARE YOU SURE you're okay?" I asked Iggy as soon as he and Jaxson returned after being outside for a few minutes.

"No, I'm not okay. I'm mad." Iggy pranced right past me and hid under the sofa.

Jaxson shrugged. "About half of the plant was decimated. Not only was Iggy upset, I was, too."

"What kind of animal ate it?"

"I'm guessing the seagulls, but it might have been bugs. Considering all of the squawking we heard, I have to agree with Iggy that it probably was his favorite bird." He showed me the pictures, and my heart sank.

"If I didn't think it would harm Iggy, I'd suggest we spray the plant, not that I know of anything that would deter seagulls. Since that's not an option, I'll just buy another plant. Maybe if we have enough bushes, some will survive."

"Sounds good."

Jaxson leaned closer. "Iggy wants to have a feeder that dispenses Alka Seltzer for the seagulls."

I was horrified. "While helpful to humans, those pellets will harm the birds, or worse, kill them, or so I've heard." I wonder how Iggy found out about that.

"Don't worry, I told him no."

"Good. I'm hoping if we involve him in our case, he'll forget about Tippy." I made sure to keep my voice low.

A half smile crossed his face. "Good luck with that."

Wasn't that the truth? "On a different note, I'm about to come up with a list as to who might have killed Irene. Want to help?"

"Of course." His only other option would have been to leave the office.

To make this easier on us all, I sat on the sofa and placed the white board on my lap. I then drew three vertical lines. On the top of the column, I listed suspect, then motive, and finally age since Jaxson thought that a really old person wouldn't be driving at night.

Penny, Rihanna, and Jaxson had been through my process of find-the-killer before. "Suggestions?" I placed the board on the coffee table for all to see.

"I know you don't want to put her name down, but you have to list Agnes," Rihanna said.

Trying not to judge, I wrote down her name, because we had heard some compelling arguments to indicate she might have killed Sally. "Motive? I personally don't have one since Agnes seemed to like both Adam and Irene."

"If Adam pointed a finger at Agnes six years ago, he must have based it on something," Rihanna said.

"That makes sense, but why did he claim that? Could Agnes have decided that since her husband was dead and Adam was rich, that she'd see if he was interested in a dalliance? The only way for that to work would be to get rid of Irene—or Sally. So what if Irene and Agnes had been friends. I know that goes against what you found out, Penny, but it could have happened."

"It's possible, but like you said, Agnes would have had to put aside her friendship with Irene to do so. It's a good theory, though." Rihanna studied me. "You're just guessing, right? Or did you hear something?" she asked.

My cousin must not be attempting to read my mind. If she had, she'd know I was shooting from the hip. "It's a guess." I turned to Penny. "You asked about Agnes. What is your take?"

"If I believed her friends, Agnes should be sainted."

"Why again is that?" I asked. "She stalked someone."

"Other than that, when she was alive, she'd always bake a meal for someone if that person was down. The neighbor said she would volunteer for different charities all the time."

"Hmm. That doesn't seem like the actions of a killer, but who knows? Maybe she snapped one day. For the sake of completeness, we'll put her name down." I wrote the motive as jealousy, and age as too old to drive at night, which kind of discounted her as Irene's killer. Sally's death was still open. "If Agnes was too old to drive, I suppose she could have hired someone to take out Irene." I wanted to be fair. "What number should we assign to her." In case Penny forgot the system, I told her to rank the likelihood from one to ten."

"A two," she said.

"I'd give her a five," Rihanna said.

I looked over at Jaxson. "You?"

"Go with four."

"That's a nice compromise. Next?"

"Adam Talbert," Jaxson said. "I believe the town's consensus was that he killed his wife. Motive might be that Irene decided she didn't want to give him a divorce—assuming they were that far along in the process—and since Adam wanted Sally, he'd need Irene out of the way. It's why I'd give Adam a six."

"Sounds good." For age, I put late seventies. "I'm thinking he wasn't driving, but if he was rich, he, too, could have hired someone to run over his wife." When no one contradicted me, I continued. "Anyone else?"

"You have to put down Irene's name. If she was as upset about the break up as Miriam implied, she might have tried to commit suicide," Rihanna offered.

"We can't discount that possibility. I'll put depression/suicide as the motive. If she did hire someone, we have no idea who that would be unless Sheriff Duncan had asked for phone records. This almost makes it the perfect crime. Ranking for this option?"

"Three, since Miriam didn't really have any proof," Rihanna said.

I didn't mention that we didn't have proof for any of them. When no one complained, I jotted down her suggestion. I looked around, waiting for another suggestion, but the three of them seemed without any other ideas.

"What about Sally?" Iggy said, emerging from under the sofa.

I was thrilled that Iggy wanted to participate after the Tippy attack. "That's an excellent suggestion. Thank you. Motive?"

"Maybe she heard that Irene wanted to get back with her husband, and Sally didn't want to give up the nice lifestyle."

"I have to say that has potential." I would tell him anything if only to encourage Iggy to forget about that stupid seagull. I wrote down Sally's name. Six years ago, she would have been in early sixties or late fifties, assuming Jean Elkhart was a good guesser of age. That meant Sally could have been driving the car that night. "Ranking?"

"Seven," Iggy said.

He would give his suggestion the highest number. Part of me was happy that he didn't suggest Tippy had killed Irene, though I doubt driving was one of a seagull's skills. "Anyone else?"

"Unless you think another one of the other ghosts killed Irene—when they were alive, of course—then no," Jaxson said.

"For now, this is a good start. Speaking of the other ghosts, we need to know more about Gladys, Wes, and Neil." I turned to Penny. "Great job on uncovering the dirt on Agnes."

She smiled. "It was fun—much more than waitressing."

If we had enough jobs to keep her busy, I'd hire her in a heartbeat. "I agree. Did Hunter say how his search was coming on Wes?"

"He is trying to find something, but he hasn't been successful yet. I should offer to help him."

I smiled. "You do that. I want to head on over to Hex and Bones to see if Andorra has learned anything about Gladys." I turned to Iggy. "Do you want to come? Maybe you can find out from Hugo if he has a way to contact ghosts."

Iggy spun around twice, indicating his pleasure at the idea. "Yes!"

I would have asked Jaxson or Rihanna if either of them wanted to join me, but it might be nice to have it be just me and Iggy for a change. We needed time to bond.

Penny stood. "I'm out of here. I'm going to drive over to the forest for that surprise visit. If Hunter's roaming around the woods, I'll wait. I'll let you know if he learned anything."

I could tell she wanted to have an excuse to see her beau. "Great."

"I think I'll go downstairs to see what, if anything, Drake unearthed on Wes."

"Sounds good."

Jaxson had found many Neil Phillips in Florida as well as a few in our adjacent states. That meant we wouldn't be asking any neighbors about him unless we narrowed down his location. Only then could Jaxson check the obituaries to see if any of the Neil Phillips were dead in that town. One issue was that we didn't even know when Neil had passed. He could have died a hundred years ago, for all we knew.

"Mind if I join you?" Rihanna asked.

I should have realized that with her boyfriend away at school, she'd appreciate the company.

"Of course not."

With Iggy snug in my bag, we walked over to the Hex and Bones. "I should have called, but do you know if Andorra is working today?"

Rihanna shrugged. "Drake's working, so Andorra probably is, too."

"Even if she has the day off, Iggy might be able to extract some information from Hugo."

When we entered the store, I placed Iggy on the floor and

let him do his thing. Naturally, he rushed to the back to find his friend. I spotted Andorra at the counter, and as soon as she saw us, she motioned us over.

"Hey, I'm glad you're here," she said.

"I figured Iggy could use some Hugo time."

She hissed in a breath. "Hugo's not here."

I froze. "What? What happened?"

"Nothing. He and Genevieve are having some *together* time."

"I know Hugo left the store about a month ago, but is this a common occurrence now?" I asked.

"Kind of. He and Genevieve are fairly inseparable. She likes to take him out since she said he needs to learn to interact with others."

"But he's still mute, right?"

"Yes, though I wouldn't discount the possibility that Genevieve might be able to help him regain his speech."

If she could do a spell to make Hugo talk again, I would have thought she would have done it already. On the other hand, she might like that only a few people could communicate with him. "Do you know where she's taking him on this date?"

"I think they are going back to where it all began."

"The church?" I asked.

"Yes. It's sweet and all, but I miss him when he's not here. Don't worry, though. They don't stay out of sight for very long."

"Is it because he loses strength when he's away from the store?" Rihanna asked.

"I'm not sure, but maybe."

Iggy ran over. "Hugo's gone, Hugo's gone."

His pain sliced through me. I lifted him up and placed him on the counter so we could talk more easily. "He's not really gone. He and Genevieve are on a date."

"As in a date, date?"

I chuckled. "Yes."

"Blah." He stuck out his tongue.

"Are you against romance or something? You and Aimee are an item."

"Not anymore."

"Not anymore? What happened? And why didn't you tell me?" Most likely this was a temporary setback. They'd broken up before. If it had been a serious split, Aunt Fern would have mentioned it, since I'm sure Aimee would have confided in her.

"I didn't tell you, because it's not a big deal. I'm just not interested anymore. Aimee is no longer the woman for me."

"Is that so? What happened?" I had to keep a straight face throughout this conversation.

"She doesn't understand why Tippy bothers me. Aimee keeps saying that to act afraid is to let Tippy win."

I had to agree with Aimee, but I didn't think telling that to him would help the cause. I understood that obsessive behavior could drive a loved one away, and Iggy had been focused solely on this seagull of late. "She'll come around."

"It's too late for us." He dragged a claw down his snout, probably looking for sympathy.

I hoped he was exaggerating. "You could try asking Aimee how her day was instead of focusing on the menacing seagulls. They poop on cats too, you know."

"I told her that."

I really liked that Iggy had someone to confide in—or rather had someone in the past to confide in. "Why don't you ask for her help with dealing with Tippy?"

He looked up at me. "What can she do?"

What could she do? I had to come up with something. "If she's not bothered by the gulls, maybe she's figured out how to keep them away. You should ask her."

Iggy seemed to think about it. "Maybe, but if she hisses at them, then I'm out of luck."

"You have a wicked tail swipe."

"Whatever."

He didn't seem to want to listen to other options, so I returned my attention to Andorra. "Did you find out anything about Gladys?"

"I think so. I was just going to call you, in fact."

That sounded promising. I looked around to see if anyone needed her help. Since her cousin Elizabeth was stocking some items in the aisle, she could take care of their questions.

"I first stopped off at the sheriff's office to see if Pearl knew Gladys, but she didn't since I didn't have her last name. I figured if Gladys was friends with your grandmother, she would have lived nearby. I was wrong. Determined to find her, I spread out, starting with Palm Ridge." She smiled, "And I got lucky."

"Fantastic."

"It only took a few well-placed questions to learn that Gladys' real name was Gladys Stein. Once I knew her name, it was easy to find out that her house had recently been put up for sale." She held up a hand. "I didn't ask when Gladys died, but her husband passed away about a month ago."

"That's a shame. I wonder if she knows that."

"If her husband is a warlock, they might be reunited," Rihanna said.

"Good point. Andorra, you said you learned something that might point to who murdered Irene?"

She nodded. "I'll admit this is a long shot, but according to one of Gladys' friends, who is rather old, Gladys was furious when Irene died."

"Furious or sad? There's a difference."

Andorra smiled. "That's the good part. I think furious, because she claimed a man that Gladys disliked killed Irene."

Now she had my attention. "Who?"

"His name is Harper Stiltman. He is, or rather, was business partners with Adam Talbert."

"I got ya so far," Iggy said.

I almost laughed since I hadn't realized Iggy was even paying attention.

"Why him?" I asked.

"Harper Stiltman accused Adam of stealing company funds."

Rihanna's brows rose. "Considering how wealthy Adam is, I can believe it."

I wasn't ready to make that judgment yet. "Did this friend have any proof—like accounting ledgers or anything?"

"Not that I know of."

That seemed thin then. "Even if Adam Talbert stole from his partner, why would Harper Stiltman want to kill Irene? If he had murder on his mind, why not go after Adam—or would that look too obvious?"

"That I don't know, but I got the sense there is a lot more to the story than what this woman recalled. In fact, she kept referring to Gladys in the present."

Which meant she might not be totally mentally alert. "Are you sure you have the right Gladys?"

"I can't be positive."

"It has to be her," Rihanna said.

"Why is that?"

"This Gladys spoke of Irene's husband, Adam, so Andorra must have found the correct one."

"You're right. Again." That made me feel better that we'd learned something about our other female ghost.

The door to the store opened, and who should walk in like two ordinary humans but Genevieve and Hugo. That begged the question why didn't they just teleport to the back room? Did they actually walk from the church to here? It was a good mile.

"Hugo!" Iggy called.

What I would label a smile formed on Hugo's face. He came over and picked up Iggy.

"Hugo is happy to see Iggy," Andorra said. Hugo had to have her translate since neither Rihanna nor I could communicate with him telepathically like the other three could.

Since Iggy needed his friend time, I asked Andorra if he could stay here for a bit. "I want to see if Drake has uncovered any information on Wes."

"Of course. No need to rush back," she said.

Genevieve faced us. "While Hugo and I were at the church, we noticed that the missing gargoyle has been replaced. It's ordinary stone, but it will do."

"The poor minister. He never did find out what really happened." Even if we told him, he'd never believe us.

"It's better that way," Andorra said.

Hugo tugged on Genevieve's arm, clearly wanting to get to his quiet space.

"I'll make sure those two behave," Genevieve said as she followed Iggy and Hugo into the back room.

"Thanks." I turned my attention back to Andorra. "I forgot to ask. Did you ever ask Hugo and Genevieve if they knew anything about the afterlife?"

Chapter Ten

"YES, I REMEMBERED to ask our resident gargoyle shifters about life after death. I know, I know. I should have called right away, but I got busy with Gladys," Andorra said.

"That's okay. What did they say?" If they sat on top of a church all those years, they might have met a few ghosts in their day.

"They have both interacted with those who've passed over."

That was so exciting. "What did they learn?"

"A few people who went to church regularly always looked up at the statues of Genevieve or Hugo, though after Hugo became my familiar, it was only Genevieve. When these parishioners passed over, they must have sensed a connection with her, because they visited a few times."

"That's not what I expected to hear, especially if they hadn't interacted before," I said, "but go on."

"Genevieve claimed she emitted some kind of signal to let people know she was real, but even she isn't certain that's what made them approach her."

"Let say that's true, and these ghosts visited her, what did they say about the hereafter?" I asked.

"Genevieve got the sense that not all people go to the

same place."

"I wonder if she was talking about the traditional Heaven versus the witch Nirvana or a darker, hotter place?" Of course, the image of burning fire might not be true at all.

"I couldn't say."

"Did she mention if any of these ghosts had magical powers?" That might make a difference.

"Like us, I don't think she can tell."

I wasn't ready to discount Genevieve's and Hugo's ability to help with this case. "Is it possible they both have abilities, even if they aren't aware they possess them?"

Andorra shrugged. "Anything's possible. Remember, I never knew Hugo could freeze things."

"True. If they remember something about what it's like up there, let me know."

She smiled. "Will do, and say hi to Drake for me."

"For sure."

Rihanna and I returned to the wine and cheese store. On the off chance Jaxson was downstairs with his brother, we headed to the back and entered. To my delight, they were both there. I placed my hands on his shoulders and squeezed, "Hello, guys."

Jaxson looked over his shoulder and smiled. "Hey there, what did you two find out?"

Jaxson was sitting at the prep table watching Drake create his wine and cheese baskets. I told him about Gladys Stein pointing a finger at Adam Talbert's business partner, Harper Stiltman, as the potential killer.

"Why would he kill Irene?" Drake asked.

"We don't know. I'm guessing he was angry at Adam for

stealing company money."

"Why not just kill Adam?" Jaxson asked.

"I wondered that myself. I'd be guessing here, but killing Adam's wife would bring the man a lot of pain and guilt."

"Is this Harper Stiltman still alive?" Jaxson asked.

"I don't know. So many have passed that I guess I assumed he had."

"Do you know what business they were engaged in?" Jaxson asked.

"No." Clearly, I was off my game today. "Sorry."

"I'll do a little research." He turned to his brother and did a fist bump. "Later, bro."

"Did you learn anything about Wes?" I asked Drake.

"Not yet, but I have a few more calls to make. I'll let you know what I find out."

"I appreciate it."

The three of us went upstairs. While Jaxson headed to his desk, I pulled out the white board. "I need to add one more name."

"Do you really think this business partner could have killed Irene?" Rihanna asked.

"I'm not making any judgments. I'm merely the scribe. Eventually, more facts will turn up that will narrow the field." I wrote down Stiltman's name and added revenge as the motive. I put Gladys Stein's name in parentheses so we'd know where the clue came from. "Any guess what his ranking should be?"

"Maybe a three," Rihanna said. "I just don't see him as a front runner."

"Me neither." But I'd been wrong before.

"Got something," Jaxson said.

"That was fast." Rihanna and I stepped over to his computer. "What did you find?"

"According to one site, Harper Stiltman and Adam Talbert were owners in a cleaning products business. There is no mention of Mr. Stiltman being dead, but the article is old."

"I'll call Pearl. She might know him."

"Do that, and I'll keep looking."

I returned to the sofa and called my top gossip queen. Since it was after three, her shift at the sheriff's department would have ended, so I contacted her on her home phone.

"Glinda?" Pearl sounded a little out of breath.

"Yes, it's me. Can I ask you something?"

"Of course."

"Do you know a Harper Stiltman?"

She said nothing for a moment. Most likely Pearl had to dig deep into her memory. "I know him."

I couldn't tell what that meant. "Is he still alive?"

"If you can call it that."

What was up with her today? "What do you mean?"

"After Irene Talbert died, he retired, or maybe I should say, he became a hermit. I don't know of anyone who has seen or heard from him since. I know he sold the company, though."

I wonder how she'd learned Irene's last name? It must have been the grapevine at work. "Do you know if he lives in town?"

"Rumor has it that he lives on some farm with his cows."

I wanted to give her a bit of gossip to see how she responded. "I heard that he and Adam Talbert, his business partner, had a falling out."

"I heard that, too."

I waited for Pearl to give me more information, but she remained silent, which wasn't like her. "Did you hear that Stiltman accused Adam of stealing company money?"

"I did, but then the whole thing died down when Harper's wife became ill and passed quickly."

No wonder he let the issue drop. "I appreciate the intel."

"By the way, I'm still looking into those names you asked me about."

"That's good. I found out that Gladys Chipper is actually Gladys Stein, and that she lived in Palm River."

"I didn't know that, but I'll make a note."

About the only ones we had nothing on were Wes and Neil, though maybe Drake or Hunter would uncover something on Wes. I decided not to tell her anything else that we'd learned, since I didn't want to prejudice her investigation.

I disconnected and told them what Pearl said. I then turned to Rihanna. "I don't know how you'd know, but any idea how to find a recluse who lives on a farm?"

She chuckled. "Not a clue."

"Hmm. I could use a little something to eat," I said. "Want to head over to the Tiki Hut and pick Aunt Fern's brain? Afterward, we can get Iggy."

"Sounds like a plan."

"Jaxson, do you want to join us?"

He swiveled around. "If you don't mind, I want to see what I can find on their company."

"Okay. I can get you something at the restaurant if you

want."

"I'm good, but thanks."

Rihanna and I left and walked over to my aunt's restaurant. As much as I would have liked something to eat, when I noticed someone else was manning the cashier counter, I motioned that we go upstairs. I knocked on Aunt Fern's door. When she answered, she didn't act surprised. Had the rumor mill—read Pearl—been at work already?

"Come in, come in. You won't learn anything standing in the hallway."

I loved my Aunt Fern. She was a hoot. When I went in, I was greeted by her cat, Aimee, as well as Iggy.

"What are you doing here? I thought you were with Hugo."

"Hugo and Genevieve had to do something, so they carried me over here."

I looked up at Aunt Fern to make sure that was the truth. "They did," she said.

I would have thought that Iggy would have gone into our apartment, especially since he said he and Aimee had recently broken up. Had they repaired their relationship already?

"Hello, Aimee. How's it going?"

The cat looked up at me. "I told Iggy that he can't talk about Tippy when he is with me. That's all."

I hadn't asked, but Iggy must have told her about our discussion. I wondered how long that would last, but that was none of my business. "Good to know." I turned to my aunt. "I was wondering if you remember a Harper Stiltman?"

"Of course, I do. He and Irene's husband, Adam, were business partners. Have a seat, and I'll get you something to drink. Then we can chat."

There was no use telling her I'd rather talk than have a drink. My aunt was the consummate hostess. Rihanna and I sat next to each other on the sofa, and Aimee jumped up between us, clearly wanting some attention. I looked over at Iggy to see his response, but he turned his back and waddled after Aunt Fern. So much for returning to paradise.

My aunt returned shortly carrying a tray containing two sweet teas and a plate of chocolate chip cookies that smelled fresh from the oven. I inhaled and moaned. "You sure do know what I like."

"I do." She set the tray on the coffee table and then sat down. "Why do you want to know about Harper?"

"Andorra found information on one of the ghosts—a Gladys Stein. Her neighbors claimed that Gladys thought that Harper killed Irene."

I waited for my aunt to either agree or disagree. "I can see Gladys thinking that, but Harper isn't a killer."

That was a lot of information in a few words. "To be clear, you know Gladys Stein?"

"Oh, yes. She lived over in Palm Ridge. We didn't socialize much, but I knew her. She and your grandmother would come into the restaurant at times."

Who knew? "Let's start with why you believe Gladys Stein would think Harper could be responsible for Irene's death?"

"She never liked Harper. To give you a little background, Harper and Adam owned a cleaning supply company. They both went into the company as equal partners, but Harper acted like whatever he said was the final word."

The information about them owning a cleaning supply

company matched what Jaxson had found. "That could create some tension, but I don't see what this has to do with Irene or Gladys." I munched on a cookie. Oh, my. The sweet confection helped calm me. I then washed it down with a perfectly sweetened iced tea. Aunt Fern knew just the right amount of sugar to use.

"I heard your grandmother comment that Irene made no bones about the fact that she didn't like Harper since he was always picking on her husband. Since Gladys and Irene were good friends, she took Irene's side. Don't ask how they came to be friends in the first place. That I don't know."

"Interesting. That paints Adam as a weak man," I said.

"He was. I believe that was a bone of contention between Irene and Adam."

That was a new twist. "Not the fact that Adam was seeing another woman?"

Aunt Fern's eyes widened. "Oh, my. I hadn't heard about that. What do you know?"

I told her what their neighbor had said about the floozy stopping over at the Talbert's house once Irene moved out. I followed up by telling her that Priscilla said that Sally Gentran and Adam were having an affair.

"I had no idea. I must be slipping."

"Hardly. Besides, that happened years ago. Not only that, these women weren't in your inner circle."

"No, I suppose not."

"Now that you're kind of caught up, let's get back to Harper. According to Andorra, Harper believed that Adam was stealing from the company."

Aimee jumped off the sofa. "Here, I thought I had problems."

What did that mean?

"Unlike your Nana, I wasn't close to Irene," Aunt Fern said. "So, I can't say what is true and what is not."

"Could Irene have confronted Harper about accusing her husband of cheating?" Rihanna asked. "If so, Harper might have decided to do away with her, though I'm not sure how Irene could have harmed Harper either emotionally or financially."

"She was a witch," I said. "Who knows what she could have done?"

"That's true," Aunt Fern said. "All I know is that Harper's wife, Elaine, had a bad heart, and that she died shortly before Irene did."

There had to be a connection there someplace. "I wonder if all of the squabbling created so much stress that it caused Elaine's heart to fail. I know I have no facts to back this up, but maybe Harper thought it was all Adam's fault."

My aunt nodded. "That could be. Wanting to get back at Adam, Harper killed his wife. Tit for tat, so to speak."

Speculation was all well and good, but we needed more. "Do you know of anyone who knew Harper well?"

"I don't think anyone knew Harper Stiltman well."

"What about the people who worked at their company?" This came from Iggy who seemed to suddenly become interested in the case once more.

"I don't know who they were," Aunt Fern said, "but I would have Pearl or Gertrude ask around. It happened more in their time."

"Good idea. Do you know where this cleaning company

was located?"

"Believe it or not, I never shopped there. I know it was closer to Summertime than Witch's Cove. I'd ask your friend Delilah at the library to find some articles about that time. I recall they had a grand opening many, many years ago. That might show pictures of the employees."

I grinned. "You are brilliant."

"Hardly. I'm just old."

We all laughed. I finished most of the cookies and my drink. "Iggy, do you want me to drop you off at the office, or do you want to stay here?"

"I'll stay here."

Hopefully, Aimee had been able to give him some tactics on how to foil Tippy.

Rihanna and I walked back to the office where we found Drake and Jaxson upstairs. Drake's assistant, Trace, must be tending to the store.

"Hey, guys. I hope you have news," I said.

"I do, but you first," Drake said.

How did he know I knew something? Never mind. Drake always could read me—as could his brother. I detailed what Andorra told us about Gladys Chipper aka Gladys Stein and her belief that Adam Talbert's business partner killed Irene.

"Wow. That is some information," Drake said. "Did she learn why Gladys believed Harper Stiltman was the murderer?"

"No, and none of the neighbors seemed to know either. I spoke with Aunt Fern, and she knew both of them, but she could only guess. According to a few sources, Harper Stiltman is kind of a recluse. He lives somewhere outside of town on a farm."

"I can work with that," Jaxson said. "Anything else?"

"I plan to hit up Delilah at the library to see what she can find out about this cleaning supply company these men ran. I'd like to locate some employees so I can find the dirt on these two men."

"Sounds good."

I turned to Drake. "You said you learned something about Wes Armstrong?"

"I did."

Chapter Eleven

WES ARMSTRONG HAD seemed interested in my grandmother, but I hadn't heard he was friends with either Irene or Adam. "Tell me what you found out."

"I managed to get a hold of a few neighbors who remembered Wes. Most kind of felt sorry for the guy. Apparently, he liked his women and his booze a little too much," Drake said. "I didn't get the name of any bars he frequented, but someone might remember where he hung out."

"There aren't many bars in Witch's Cove, so I wouldn't be surprised if he went to some of the neighboring towns. Drake, did these neighbors say anything about Wes liking my grandmother?"

He shook his head. "I only learned that he passed about three years ago and was no youngster—mid seventies I'd say. From what I could tell, the man was lonely and would talk to anyone who would listen."

That was sad. "Yet he was one of the four ghosts who appeared to us."

"All I can say is that no one I spoke with even hinted that Wes was dangerous or that he might have harmed Irene or anyone else for that matter."

"That is good intel."

"Thanks."

"Now that we'd learned about three of the four ghosts, I need to think what my next move will be," I said.

"How about seeing if Pearl knows anything about this cleaning company?" Rihanna suggested.

"Good idea." I pulled out my phone, and I called her. Again.

"Well, isn't this getting to be a regular event? I like it," Pearl said.

"I hope I'm not bothering you too much, but do you remember a cleaning supply company run by Harper Stiltman and Adam Talbert?"

"Sure do. They had the best supplies around. I was really sad when they closed."

"Do you remember the name of their company?" I crossed my fingers.

"It hasn't been that long ago. It was Stiltman's."

That was an odd choice of names. "Not Stiltman's and Talbert's?"

"I heard the longer name wouldn't fit on their sign."

That seemed rather weak. I didn't ask why they didn't name it Talberts. That was an easier name to spell anyway. "Do you remember anyone who worked there?"

She didn't say anything for a bit. "The one or two I remember aren't with us anymore."

"That's too bad."

"It is. Anything else I can help you with?" Pearl seemed to want to continue chatting. She did love people—and gossip.

"Not at the moment, but I'll call if I have any further questions."

"You do that. I'm always here."

"Thanks. Bye." Not that I wasn't happy with all of this new information, but I wasn't sure how it could help us. I told Jaxson the name of the store.

"Not too original, is it?" he said.

"No, but small towns like businesses that carry a family name."

"Then the Tiki Hut Grill should have been called Goodall's Grill."

I smiled. "Maybe, but that's not Aunt Fern's style."

"You said you were going to touch base with Delilah. Are you still going to speak with her?" he asked.

"I am. Aunt Fern thought we might be able to find some old articles that included the names or pictures of some of the employees."

Jaxson shifted in his chair. "If you find these people, are you planning to ask about the feud between Harper and Adam?"

"Why not? It seems like a good thing to know."

"I agree," he said.

I texted Delilah to see if she was working tonight at the library. While I could have just asked her to locate the information for me, like she'd done several times before, I wasn't exactly sure what I wanted to know. Going in person would be better, especially if there were photos to view.

Less than five minutes later, she returned my text stating that she was indeed there.

Great. See you soon, I texted back. "Anyone want to join me?" I asked.

"I'd like to, but I think we're better off if I stay and do

some investigating here," Jaxson said.

Rihanna waved. "I'll go."

"Great." I didn't think Delilah would lie about anything, but someone there might.

I grabbed my purse and motioned Rihanna to join me. I drove since the library was on the far edge of town. Once inside the vast volumes of book collections, I headed to the circulation desk where Delilah was working.

She looked up and smiled. "This is such a treat to see both of you again. How have you been doing?"

I didn't know where to begin. "We're doing great."

We chatted for about ten minutes, but eventually my patience got the best of me. "I do have a favor to ask."

She smiled. "Tell me."

I explained that I was interested in the history of Stiltman's. "They made cleaning supplies, though I honestly don't know when they closed exactly."

"That should be easy to find. The library is good about keeping all things that relate to Witch's Cove and the county in general. To be honest, every time I look through the articles, I get lost in the past. Our history is fascinating."

It was refreshing to find someone who loved her job so much. "Where do we begin?"

"Let's step over to our historical section."

I had no idea the town had one. "Show me the way."

In the back of the library was a section filled with old photos, shelves of assorted books, and a computer that I suspected was for research. In addition, there was a microfiche machine that could display old newspaper articles. That would be useful, assuming the company was around back then.

"How about if each of us take a different area to search?" Delilah suggested.

"Sounds wonderful," I said.

Rihanna wanted to study the photographs, which could prove very useful should we ever meet Mr. Stiltman. I set to work on the old newspaper articles about the town, and Delilah searched the database.

"If anyone comes across the location of Mr. Stiltman's farm, let me know," I said.

It only seemed like a few minutes had passed—actually it had been an hour—when I spotted an article on the opening of their building. From the angle of the shot of the store, I couldn't quite tell its location. However, several employees, along with their names, were listed. Knowing that could prove very helpful. I took several snapshots with my phone, hoping Jaxson could find these folk.

Rihanna returned with some screen captures of old photos. "I think I found Mr. Stiltman's farm. Actually, I found the farm, just not the exact location, but someone with a knowledge of the area might be able to tell where it is."

"Great find."

We spent another hour pouring over the history of Witch's Cove. "Delilah, this information is a town treasure."

She smiled. "I think so too."

Once I believed we'd found all that we could, we thanked Delilah again and left. Had I not been starving, I might have stayed until the library closed. This information fascinated me.

In the car I asked if Rihanna was hungry. *Please say yes.*

"Always. Which gossip center should we hit up?"

I could always ask Aunt Fern questions. "I'm not sure. Dolly didn't know our ghosts, but she might know something about the cleaning supply company or Stiltman's farm."

"Then the diner it is. Do you want me to call Jaxson and ask him to join us?"

She knew the routine well. "That would be great."

By the time I parked at the diner, my stomach was grumbling. To my delight, Jaxson was already there with an almost empty glass of soda. He smiled and waved from one of the booths in back.

I slid in next to him. "Hey."

"You two were gone a while." He didn't sound like he was complaining, just curious.

"We were, but we have information."

"I'm glad one of us was successful."

Before I could tell him what we'd found, Dolly rushed over. "Hello, you guys. How's the hunt for your friend?"

I had to assume that Pearl had filled her in. "We're narrowing down who might have murdered Irene, but we don't have a main suspect yet."

"I see."

"Do you remember a store by the name of Stiltman's?"

"Of course, I do."

I did a mental fist pump. "Where is it located?"

"It was on Parish Road, near the intersection with Holland Avenue."

Not being great with directions, I pulled out my phone and did a search. When I found the place, I put the little Google man on the area and held it up to her. "Can you tell me exactly where it is?"

Dolly bent over and studied it. "The building is gone now. Some developers put up an apartment building in its place. But here is where it used to be." She pointed to the area.

"That is a shame."

"It is."

"Do you remember anyone who might know who worked there?" Rihanna asked.

We had some names, but if Dolly knew anyone personally, she might pave the way for us to speak with that person.

Dolly straightened. "Not personally, but I bet I could find out." She almost giggled. "Let me take your order, and I'll make a call."

"You are the best." The three of us told her what we wanted to eat.

As soon as she left, a sense of relief washed over me. "I think we may crack this case after all." I know I've said that before, but I could feel it in my bones that we were close.

"I hope so, but suppose you learn that a Jane Smith worked at the store," Jaxson said. "Do you think she'd be aware of the conflict between her two bosses?"

I stuck my tongue out at him. "Maybe not, but if we don't ask, we won't find out."

Jaxson smiled. "Way to have a positive attitude."

Another server delivered our drinks, promising our meals would be out shortly. While the diner did have excellent service, it's best trait was its gossip.

"What did you learn?" I asked Jaxson.

"Like I said, not much. I found an old article that someone never took down that showed what they sold at Stiltman's but that's all. No date of closure or anything."

"Everyone is giving us a lot of information—much of which seems to be contradictory, and I can't seem to keep things straight. I swear my memory is getting worse."

He laughed. "It's called overload. Every night you should write down what you learned that day. We could keep a file in the cloud that we all have access to. Any time anyone learns anything, he or she can add to the information."

My mouth half opened. "That's a brilliant idea. Why haven't we done it before?"

Jaxson grinned. "I don't know."

The burden of having to remember everything lifted off of me. I turned to my cousin. "I've been so embroiled in the case for the last two days that I haven't even asked how Gavin is settling into school."

Rihanna smiled. "He's fine, but of course, he misses me."

"As he should. When are you going to see him again?"

She blew out a breath. "We are working on that."

"Good for you." Considering her very rough start in life, I couldn't be more thrilled that she'd landed on her feet. Rihanna was like the sister I never had.

Dolly hurried over with a big grin on her face and placed a piece of paper on the table. "You won't believe this. Sierra actually knows the woman who did all of the books for the Stiltman company."

I had no idea who Sierra was, but I suppose it didn't matter as long as her information was accurate. I wanted to ask if this bookkeeper was still alive, but I figured she must be. "That's amazing. Do you think she'd be willing to talk with us?"

"Sierra says that she's a really nice person. Her name is Mary Denfield, and she lives over in Summertime."

"This is fantastic. I'll contact her tomorrow."

Dolly grinned. "Happy to help."

She might have given us the final clue to this mystery. I tucked the paper in my purse. "As their bookkeeper, this woman might be able to shed some light on the altercation between Harper Stiltman and Adam Talbert."

"Let's hope, but their fight might be about the missing funds," Jaxson said.

"If Adam did steal some money, why did he do it? That would be important to know."

After we went round and round about his possible reasons, we finished eating, and then we each headed home. I promised to contact Mary first thing in the morning to set up a time for us to visit—assuming she was willing and able to talk to us.

When I walked into my apartment, Iggy was on his stool wearing something rather strange.

"What do you have on?"

"Aunt Fern is amazing. It took her less than an hour to make me a cape to protect me against you-know-who."

"Are you going to sleep in that?" The hood was tied under his chin, and it had a strap that went under his body. It didn't look all that comfortable.

"No. Maybe you can take it off. I'm safe from Tippy in here."

"Sure." I removed the cape and placed it next to him. "You don't think Tippy will think you are afraid of him if he sees you in this?"

Iggy looked up at me. "You think?" Sadly, he wasn't being sarcastic.

"I hope not, but I say give it a try. Please note that means you'll owe me big time if I have to wash the cape if the seagulls target you."

"You might be right. I'll sleep on it."

I smiled. Iggy was one of the lights in my life. "You do that."

Chapter Twelve

"HOW DID MARY sound when you called her?" Jaxson asked the next morning at the office.

"Relieved, maybe? It was as if she's wanted to get something off her chest for a while now." I realize I was probably projecting what I wanted her to say, but it might be true.

His brows rose. "What did you tell her about why you were calling?"

"I said that you and I ran the Pink Iguana Sleuth Agency and were looking into the cold case of Irene Talbert."

He whistled. "Not beating around the bush, are you?"

"Not my style. Ready to see if she is willing to spill her guts?"

"Sure." He looked around the office. "Where's Iggy?"

"He said he wanted to stay at the apartment. Either he wants to try to get into Aimee's better graces, or he's up to something."

"You said your aunt made him a cape? Was he wearing it when you left?"

"Yes. Why does that matter?"

"Could he be planning to ask Hugo to help us somehow with the case? And he needs the cape to protect himself from Tippy when he crosses the street?"

"I hope not. He knows he's not supposed to do that. Then again, Iggy hasn't been acting like himself of late. Because of the mess with his nemesis, I honestly thought he wasn't all that interested in finding out who'd killed Irene, but maybe I'm wrong."

"Maybe, maybe not. Do you have Mary's address?" he asked.

I smiled. "I do."

Since Rihanna wanted to spend the day taking pictures, Jaxson had told her we'd catch up later. She promised that if Iggy got in a snit, or was bombed by Tippy, that she'd take care of him. I had the best cousin.

Jaxson drove. "How are you going to approach the Talbert-Stiltman issue?" he asked.

"I'm not sure, but I won't be saying that four ghosts came to me claiming that my dead grandmother was worried because Irene Talbert—also a dead woman—was missing."

"You don't want her to think you're crazy?"

"Ah, no."

He looked over at me and smiled. "How about we say we are working with the sheriff's department, and he asked for our help in doing some legwork on a few cold cases?"

"That works. I can even show her our card to prove we run our own agency, even though we aren't working for Steve." I tried not to lie whenever possible.

"I know, but let's hope if Mary Denfield wants to unburden her soul, we might not have to say much of anything."

I liked that approach. "Let's hope."

Mary lived outside of Summertime, not far from Witch's Cove, in a home that was rather upscale. I guess I'd thought that when Stiltman's closed, she might have struggled financially and that she'd be living elsewhere. Being a bookkeeper, she probably had found other work—or so I hoped.

We pulled into her driveway, and when I got out, my skin tingled in anticipation. Mary could be the key to this entire case. And yes, I'd thought that a few times before.

I knocked, and an elegantly, well-dressed woman wearing large dangly earrings answered. She was tall and thin with light blonde hair and perfect makeup. Of all the images I had of Mary Denfield, she didn't meet any of them, in part because this woman couldn't have been more than forty.

"Mary?" I asked.

"No, that's my mother. Glinda, I presume?"

"Yes."

"She's expecting you. Come in."

This woman led us into a rather dark living room. A woman in her seventies or maybe eighties was in a lounge chair with an afghan draped across her lap. Considering it was warm in the house, I was surprised she needed the blanket, unless she was a bit cold-blooded. That, or it was there to give her comfort.

"Can I get you two anything to drink?" Mary's daughter asked.

"No, thank you."

"Mom, ring the bell if you need me."

Mary smiled. "Thank you, Bella." She studied us for a moment. "Have a seat you two. It's not often that I get company these days."

We took the proffered sofa. "I heard you worked as a

bookkeeper for Stiltman's, is that correct?" I hadn't meant to sound like a trial lawyer, but I needed to confirm that my information was correct.

"Yes, for thirty years."

"Impressive, Ms. Denfield," Jaxson began. "What can you tell us about the relationship between Mr. Stiltman and Mr. Talbert?"

Her eyebrows rose. "That would take a long time to explain fully, but I'll give you the short version." She lifted her hands out from under the blanket and wove her fingers together, probably needing time to decide what to say. "In the beginning, things were great. Harper and his lovely wife, Elaine, were friends with Irene and Adam."

That isn't surprising considering they agreed to go into business together, but something had caused a rift. "You said in the beginning. What changed?"

"The tension slowly built between the two men in part because the company was growing too fast for Adam's liking. I know that sounds like a company's dream, but Adam wanted to keep it small. He was a small town boy at heart. Harper wanted Stiltman's to be a household name in all of Florida."

"I assume they argued about it?" Jaxson asked.

She huffed. "Too often. That's when it started."

"What started?" I asked.

"The deceit. Adam thought that if Harper believed the company wasn't doing well, he wouldn't pursue future expansion."

I wasn't sure if she was referring to the supposed theft or something else. "Did Adam steal money from the company in order to make it look like they weren't doing well?"

She coughed and held up her hand. When the spell passed, she continued. "Yes. I never told anyone that, and the guilt has nearly killed me. You might wonder why I would come clean now, but the truth is, I don't have much longer to live."

My heart broke for her. "I'm sorry."

Her shoulders slumped. "It is what it is. I've learned to come to grips with it."

I didn't want to tax her too much, and she'd solved one issue we had. Now on to the next one. "Do you have any idea who might have killed Irene?"

She shook her head. "Like many people, I've heard the rumors about it being Adam, but I know it wasn't him. He loved Irene. He never would have harmed her."

That didn't jive with what we'd learned. "He was unfaithful, or so I've heard."

She sipped her glass of water. "Only after Irene and Harper…well, you can guess."

Whoa! That came out of left field. "Are you saying that Harper and Irene had an affair?" I thought she told Agnes that she didn't like him. Was that all a lie?

"Yes, and I don't say that lightly. I adored Irene. She was strong, resourceful, and quite kind, but Adam was the opposite of Harper. Harper was a strong man with a vision for the company, while Adam was not."

"Since you were the company's bookkeeper, did you help Adam cook the books?" Jaxson asked.

"I am ashamed to say that I did."

And here I thought she liked Harper more than Adam. "Why did you do it?"

She blew her nose. "I needed the money. I'd been suffering from congestive heart failure for a while, and I knew I'd need long term care. Adam promised I'd be set for life if I did this for him." She waved a hand. "He bought this house and even paid enough for me to hire my daughter to take care of me. She works from home as a law clerk."

Hence the nice clothes, not to mention the upscale home. I tried to put the rest of the pieces together, but not everything was gelling. Was the theft just about not wanting to expand? Or was it about more than that—like to make up for the fact his wife and Harper were together? "Did Adam know that Irene was cheating on him with his partner?"

"Not right away, but eventually he found out. That's when he did two things: one, steal the money to punish Harper, and two, he took up with another woman. I'd be guessing here, but I think he believed that if he was rich enough, Irene would want to come back to him."

That was some messed up stuff. "But she didn't run into Adam's arms, did she?"

Mary held up a finger. "Oh, but she did. Sort of. Mind you, that was only after Elaine became ill. Deep down, Harper was a good man. He was married and understood that it was up to him to care for his wife."

Good men didn't cheat on their wives, no matter the reason. I had the sense Mary was the one who liked Harper even though she agreed to do Adam's bidding against him.

"So, you're saying that Irene left Adam for Harper, and when he sent her on her way, she happily went back to Adam?" I wanted to be sure I hadn't misunderstood.

"It certainly wasn't happily."

At least that piece of information made sense, but so far, I was unable to figure out who might have harmed Irene. "Did Irene ever threaten Harper that she'd tell his wife if he dumped her?"

Harper might have decided to kill Irene to prevent his secret from escaping. I'd heard Elaine had died suddenly, and I wanted to check my facts. So far, the gossip queens weren't batting a thousand.

She shook her head. "Irene wouldn't have had the chance, because Elaine suffered a heart attack the day after Irene and Harper split. His wife died the next day."

That was consistent with what we'd learned, but it wouldn't hurt to take a look at that autopsy report. Irene was a witch, or so I believed, which meant some magic might have helped the heart attack along.

"What did Irene do then?" Jaxson asked.

"She did what any very smart woman would do. She wiped her hands of men and left Adam—again." Mary coughed again so hard, Bella rushed in.

"I'm sorry, but this is a bit too much for my mom."

I totally understood. We both got up. "Thank you, Mary. We will find out who killed Irene." I handed her my card. "If you think of anything."

"Yes, and thank you."

"One more thing, do you know where Harper Stiltman lives? I believe he's on his ranch somewhere near here."

"Yes." She gave us some rather vague directions that I hoped would be good enough to find him.

Jaxson and I then left. Only after he was on the road, did he glance over at me. "Not what you expected, was it?"

"Absolutely not. I think I need to go back to the office, take out a piece of paper, and draw a timeline of who was with whom and why."

He flashed me a smile. "That's my girl."

For the rest of the short drive back, I tried to remember everything Mary had told us. I had promised myself that I would record all future conversations, but I didn't have the heart to do it without telling her.

A short while later, Jaxson pulled into the parking lot in front of the office. "Do you want to grab some breakfast first?"

"Yes, but I can't."

His chin tucked in. "Are you okay?"

"Yes. Or rather no. I want to have some breakfast, but I have to write this down, or I might forget everything."

"I thought you were going to record the conversation."

"I was, but when I met her, I thought it was dishonest not to tell her," I said.

"That's nice of you."

"I hope I won't regret it," I said.

"Let's see if we can jot everything down, and then we'll eat. You don't want to interview Harper Stiltman on an empty stomach."

He knew me well. "Absolutely not."

He ruffled my hair and smiled as we reached the office steps. I quickly scanned the limited space to the side of the building and tried to figure out where I might plant some hibiscus bushes to replace the one that had been eaten. If I put a few against the side, the seagulls might not be as interested in them.

We stepped inside. "Iggy, we're home," I called but he

didn't answer.

"He still might be back at the apartment," Jaxson suggested.

"Let's hope." Since I didn't see any evidence of any kind of attack, Iggy was most likely safe.

"Can I get you some tea at least?" Jaxson asked. "You look like you could use some."

"How about a cup of coffee instead? I need the brain boost."

"One coffee coming up."

While he fixed me a cup, I grabbed a sheet of paper from the printer and then sat at my desk to list what we'd learned. I drew a line down the middle and one across to form four squares. I labeled them Irene, Adam, Harper, and Sally. Since Elaine died before Irene, she couldn't have been involved in the hit-and-run.

Jaxson leaned over, startling me. "What about Gladys?"

"Oh, yeah. I forgot about her." I divided Adam's square in half and put Gladys' name. "I'll list the facts in each one."

"And Agnes?"

"See? I need help."

He smiled. "You'll be fine. I'll finish making our cups."

I scribbled down some bullet points. A minute later, Jaxson returned with my coffee and sat next to me.

"Okay, here's what I think. Like you've mentioned, Irene grew into an independent woman who probably developed feelings for her husband's partner since he was the stronger of the two partners."

"I agree," Jaxson said.

"I don't condone her cheating, but I'm trying to keep my

prejudices out of the equation," I said.

Jaxson picked up his cup and blew across the steaming brew. "Smart. What are you going to write under Adam's name?"

"Imagine your business partner, for whatever reason, decides that he wants the name of your joint company to be his name and his name only. How would you feel?"

"I'd be upset, but Adam agreed to the name of Stiltman's Cleaning Supplies, rather than Stiltman and Talbert for some reason."

"I'm not buying the two names wouldn't fit on a sign."

Jaxson held up a hand. "I agree, but instead of getting sidetracked, we can ask Mr. Stiltman himself when we speak with him."

I was so glad I had Jaxson on my side. "Totally. Getting back to Adam Talbert, he'd have been devastated to find his wife had taken up with his partner. Being Sally was just for show or revenge, according to Mary."

He nodded. "But…if you're saying deep down that Adam wanted his wife back, then he might have killed her if she said she'd never be with him."

I could come up with ten different scenarios about what could have happened, but I had nothing to base any of them on. Nonetheless, I jotted down a couple of ideas for future reference. "If we believe Mary, Adam loved his wife too much to harm her, though his actions of taking up with Sally kind of negated that in my mind."

"Does that mean you think he might have killed her?"

"He might have." I turned to the other partner. "Thoughts on Harper being guilty?"

"He's still in the running. I know Mary said that Harper's wife died right after he broke it off with Irene, but who's to say Irene didn't threaten him when he told her he needed to take care of his wife?"

"True," I said. "But there is no reason to kill Irene if his wife had already passed, though."

"Good thinking." He tapped the paper. "What part do you think Gladys plays in all of this?"

"That's hard to say. I would like to know why Gladys disliked Harper so much. It might shed some light on what happened. I have a few unsubstantiated ideas."

"Tell me."

I took another sip of my drink. "I'm guessing if Gladys and Irene were good friends that Gladys might know everything that was going on in Irene's life. If Harper was the one who seduced Irene, Gladys might have been angry at him for ruining her friend's life."

He sat there for a minute trying to figure something out. "Gladys couldn't have been seriously angry, or she would have harmed Harper herself. If she is a witch, she could have even killed him."

"True. To leave no stone unturned, do we have any reason to think she would have harmed Irene?" I asked.

He shook his head. "No, so maybe we can take her off the list. What about Sally?"

Chapter Thirteen

"SALLY GENTRAN? NOT much is known about her, other than she enjoyed receiving gifts from Adam." I picked up my now slightly cooled cup and drained it. The rich, sweet coffee did wonders for my mental acuity. "I could go either way with her. If she believed that Irene wanted to get back with Adam, or rather if Adam wanted to turn his focus on Irene, Sally might have wanted to do away with her competition."

"Put that down."

I made a note and then read over what we had. "Even after listing everything, something is missing. I think I need food in order to think more clearly. Afterward, we can head over to Mr. Stiltman's farm, assuming we can find it. Mary's directions were a little vague."

Jaxson turned back to his computer. "Let me do a quick search using Google Earth."

I watched as he zoomed into the area that Mary told us about. "Is that it?" I pointed to a huge piece of property about ten miles from here. "I didn't even know there was that much unused land that existed around here."

"It fits the description. I say we eat and then see what we can learn."

"Perfect."

After a filling meal at the Tiki Hut, we headed out to find Harper Stiltman. To my delight, we found his farm more or less on our first attempt. The fact he'd named his estate Stiltman's Ranch made it easy—that, and Jaxson could find anything.

"I have no idea what to expect from this guy," Jaxson said. "If he is guilty of anything, he might be hostile. Recluses don't like surprise visits, you know."

"I would have called first if I'd had his number. He could slam the door in our faces, but I want to give it a try." That little pep talk was more for me than for Jaxson.

After driving down a half-mile gravel road, we parked. We were halfway to the home when the front door opened and a very tall man emerged, bathed in semi-shadow. While I couldn't make out the details of his face, I really wasn't looking. All I saw was the shotgun in his hand—aimed at us. Oh, no.

"Ah, Jaxson?"

"Don't move." He held up a hand. "Sir? We've come to ask you about Irene Talbert."

"What about her? She's dead." His voice came out cold.

Either what I was about to say would get us an engraved invitation inside or shot dead. "We know, sir. We want to find out who killed her."

I said a silent prayer: *Please don't let him be the killer.* In my heart, I didn't think he was. He cared for his sick wife. The man might have exhibited some bad moral judgment, but I didn't see him as a murderer. I hope I'd assessed his character correctly. If not, it might be the end of us.

He lowered his gun, implying he might not be guilty of killing Irene. If he had, he might have shot us.

"Who are you?" he demanded in a deep, gruff voice.

Jaxson explained our credentials, throwing in Sheriff Rocker's name for good luck. "We spoke with Mary Denfield about what happened, but we want to hear your side of the story."

He leaned his gun against the doorframe. "Might as well get out of the sun. Come on in."

That was an about-face. Now that the danger was most likely past, I looked around at the vastness of his ranch. Cows were grazing off in the distance, and the home itself was a beautiful, two-story stone edifice. Calling it a house wouldn't do it justice. It was more like a mansion.

Jaxson placed a hand on my back and led me across the huge porch and through the front door. Inside the entrance was a deliciously cool parlor that was bigger than my apartment. Once through that room was a sun lit living room that overlooked acres upon acres of farm and cattle land. A definite wow view. Nor did I expect to find it so well-decorated. It was possible it had been his wife's doing.

"Tell me what you want." Mr. Stiltman's tone had yet to soften.

Okay, this wasn't going to be easy. "Can you tell me how you and Mr. Talbert decided to start your company together?"

From the way his chin jutted in, that wasn't what he expected. "Adam was a good marketer. I wasn't. People aren't my specialty."

Like I couldn't figure that out? "That sounds like a good match." *Lame, Glinda, lame.*

"It was for a while, but it was my family's money that started the company. Adam was poor at the time, but shortly thereafter, he wanted to become more involved."

This didn't match anything we'd heard before, but now it made sense that the company would be named Stiltman's. Though to be honest, everything we'd heard—except from a fairly senile Adam—had been secondhand gossip.

"Do you think Adam killed his wife?" Jaxson asked.

Way to cut to the chase.

"I don't know. I know that I cared deeply for Irene, but I loved my wife, too. I know it was wrong, but I couldn't help myself. Irene was dynamic and strong, whereas Elaine was a homebody. There's nothing wrong with that, but later in life, I wanted someone I could share my dreams with. That was Irene."

Once more I was blown away. I hadn't expected those deep, emotional observations from the likes of Stiltman—a self-professed introvert. "Did Irene ever threaten to tell your wife about you two?"

"Never. If she had, Elaine might have told Adam what Irene was up to." He motioned to the sofa. "Sit down. Please."

We took the sofa, while Harper, sat in a large, high-backed chair. "You don't think Adam knew about you and Irene then?" I asked.

"Not at first, but he found out eventually. Look, this isn't getting us anywhere. I didn't kill Irene if that is what you want to know."

Everyone claimed they were innocent.

"Is it possible that Irene took her own life?" Jaxson asked. "I know she was involved in a hit-and-run, but would she have hired someone to kill her? We were told she was rather depressed."

A very uncharacteristic laugh erupted out of Harper. "Irene Talbert was the last person to do something like that. And she was too strong to be depressed. Your facts are all wrong."

He sounded very sincere and might be right. Miriam and Maude Daniels weren't always correct. We needed to change gears here. "Could Agnes Lochridge have harmed Irene?" It was highly unlikely, but I wanted to cover all of our bases.

"Why would she? They were friends."

"What if Agnes was interested in Adam and wanted him for herself?"

He shook his head. "That wasn't the case. Adam told me Agnes only came to listen to him lament about him losing Irene, because he cheated on her. My partner might have been a good marketer, but he possessed a weak character. His problem was that he didn't understand Irene, so he couldn't give her what she really needed."

After that explanation, I had to say he'd probably made an A in psychology. I wanted to learn more about Adam, but I had to focus on Irene right now. "Okay, then what about Sally Gentran?" She was the only one left on the list, since we'd crossed off Gladys' name.

He shrugged. "I really didn't know her other than Adam lavished gifts on her, but that was none of my business."

"We heard Adam stole money from the company," Jaxson said.

Harper's jaw tightened. "He did."

"You didn't want to get back at him by killing his wife?"

Harper Stiltman jumped up so fast my heart spiked. "No, now get out."

Whoa! Hit a nerve much? I quickly grabbed my purse and rushed out, with Jaxson right behind me. I practically ran back to the truck and jumped in the passenger seat, making sure to lock the door, though a shotgun shell wouldn't care if the door was locked or not. Jaxson slid in a second later, jammed the key in the ignition, and took off.

My heart didn't slow until we were back on the road. "That was intense," I managed to say.

"Tell me about it. Did you record everything?"

Drat. "I think the moment I saw the gun, I forgot. I even had it all set to go. I'm sorry."

"Don't worry about it. I don't think he told us anything we didn't already know."

Jaxson was right. "Any idea where we go from here?"

"Nope."

It wouldn't be the first time we were stumped. What I really needed was a visit from one of our ghosts. I was sure that if I could question them one more time, I could figure out who'd killed Irene.

It didn't take long before we arrived back in town, but that didn't give me enough time for my hands to stop shaking or my heart to slow. When we entered the office, both Rihanna and Iggy—without his cape—were there.

"How did it go?" she asked.

"I'm still a wreck."

"What happened?"

Jaxson and I both sat down and told them about our meeting with Mary Denfield and Harper Stiltman. "It was intense. I'm not used to anyone pointing a gun at me."

"I can only imagine," Rihanna said.

"I wish I'd been there," Iggy said.

"Why is that?"

"He sounds like he could use a friend," Iggy said.

Sometimes he could be so sweet. "He probably could."

"What about that neighbor lady?" Rihanna asked. "What was her name? Jean something?"

There were so many names, I was getting confused. I stepped over to my desk and picked up the pile of papers with my notes on it. "Jean Elkhart."

"That's it. Why don't we lay out what we know and ask her opinion? Since all but two of the parties involved are dead, I don't think we'd be hurting any reputations."

Her suggestion helped settle my disheveled mind. "That's a great idea." I turned to Jaxson. "Do you want to come?"

"How about you two go, and I'll head to the nursery to pick up a few hibiscus plants? Doing something physical will help calm my nerves. I'd come with you if I thought the old lady was a threat."

"She's anything but a threat."

Jaxson looked over at Iggy. "Don't worry, buddy. We'll plant the hibiscus where old eagle-eyes won't notice them."

Iggy crawled over to Jaxson. "You're the best."

I was the one who'd thought of it, but if he wanted to worship Jaxson, that was okay by me.

Needing to solve this crime, I stood, and Rihanna joined me.

"You remember where she lives?" Jaxson asked.

"Got it right here." I patted the paper in my pocket.

The two of us left and found the home located next to where Adam and Irene used to live. Unfortunately, Jean Elkhart wasn't sitting on the porch.

"Let's hope she is home," Rihanna said.

"There's a car parked in the driveway, implying either she is home, or she has company. I hope she can spare a few minutes for us."

"If we tell her we have information about Sally, Irene, Harper, and Adam, she might take the time," Rihanna said.

"You're right."

We piled out of the car, and halfway up the driveway, the front door opened. A woman in a business suit exited, followed by a young couple.

Jean must be popular. I hope she wasn't too tired to speak with us. The woman turned around and locked the front door, which I found strange, unless she was Jean's daughter or something.

"Hello?" I said.

The pretty woman smiled, stepped off the porch and came up to us. "Hello. Can I help you?"

That was an odd thing to say. "We just wanted to talk to Jean Elkhart about a murder investigation."

"Who?"

"Jean Elkhart. She lives here."

"You must be mistaken. This home has been vacant for three months."

It was like I'd entered the twilight zone. "We just spoke with her yesterday. Older woman, gray hair, dressed rather casually?"

"I'm sorry. All of the furniture is covered, and I'm certain there have been no squatters."

Squatters? No amount of questioning would get her to change her story. "Thank you."

We definitely needed to regroup. I looked next door to make certain we had the right address. Sitting rather elegantly to the right was the Talbert estate.

Rihanna placed a hand on my arm. "Come on."

Maybe she read this woman's mind and could clear things up. I slipped into the driver's seat. "What did you hear? Or rather learn?" I asked as I started the engine.

"Nothing. The woman was a realtor who didn't want a scene in front of her clients. She was telling the truth."

"Then how do you explain Jean Elkhart?"

"I can't," Rihanna said. "She could have been trespassing."

I backed out of the driveway and took off. "Then why sit on the porch swing for all of the neighbors to see? Someone would have noticed and told her the place was for sale and to get along." My necklace heated up. "Nana?"

Rihanna turned to the backseat. "I don't see her."

I glanced into the rear view mirror. "I don't either. I hope I didn't imagine the pulse of heat from the stone."

"No, I don't think you did. Nana wants us to find out about Irene. I'm sure of it."

"I want to believe that, but who was that woman on the front porch? Let's see if Jaxson can do a search for Ms. Elkhart. Could she have lived in that house at one time and was now confused?" I asked.

"She seemed quite sharp to me."

"Me, too."

My mind tried to untangle what had happened, but it failed. When we pulled into the lot in front of our office, Jaxson was unloading two hibiscus bushes from his truck. I smiled. Iggy would be thrilled.

For a moment, I almost forgot about our failed assignment.

"Hey," he said. "You two weren't gone long. Wasn't Ms. Elkhart home?"

"It's complicated."

He set the two plants by the side of the building. "I'll plant these tomorrow. Let's go inside and you can tell me about it."

I hoped Jaxson could figure out what was going on. I trudged up the steps and entered into the office. "I'm getting a tea. Anyone want anything?"

"Tea for me, too," Rihanna said.

"I'll grab a soda right after I wash up." He held up his dirt stained hands.

Once Jaxson freshened up, he joined us. With our drinks in hand, we reconvened to the sofa area, where I explained to Jaxson about the realtor telling us that no one had lived in that house for months.

"Sounds like Ms. Elkhart was in a place where she wasn't invited," he said.

"Then how do you explain she knew the Talberts? Jean told us about Sal. How could that be?"

"Let me check if Jean was a former owner."

That made sense. "Please do."

I handed him the address and then waited. If Rihanna hadn't been with me both times, I might have thought I was losing it, again.

Chapter Fourteen

A FTER TEN MINUTES of waiting for Jaxson to come up with something, I became impatient. "No Jean Elkhart?"

"Not yet. I have the list of people who've owned the home next to the Talberts, but no Elkhart."

I wasn't sure what that meant. "Maybe she was married, got divorced, and was now using her maiden name."

He shook his head. "The last owners were Bill and Molly Black."

I looked over at Rihanna. "Do you have any ideas?"

"Nope."

"I'll keep looking," Jaxson said.

"Thanks."

Iggy barreled in through the cat door. "You have to stop him."

I had to assume that *him* meant Tippy. "What's he up to now?"

"He and two of his friends are eating the leaves and flowers off the new plant."

I looked over at Jaxson. This is getting out of hand. "Iggy, did you say or do anything to Tippy to make him come after you?"

"No, and in case you don't know, Tippy doesn't speak

English."

Or any language, I imagine—other than bird talk. I looked over at Jaxson. "Could we put a wire cage over the top of the plants you just bought?"

"I think I can hook up something."

Iggy waddled over to Jaxson. "Go now."

"Iggy," I said. "It's not nice to demand things. Jaxson already went to the store and bought the plants."

He dropped down onto his stomach. "Fine."

"Let me finish what I'm doing, buddy, and I'll see what I can do."

Iggy lifted his chest. If he could smile, I think he would have. "Thank you."

A few minutes later, Jaxson and I went downstairs and moved the bushes under the staircase. We spent the remainder of the evening chatting with Rihanna and then grabbed a bite to eat, in the hopes of making some sense of everything. Too many people had offered conflicting stories, and I didn't know who to believe.

Eventually, my body kind of lost its will to stay awake. "I'm heading home. I want to make an early night of it."

"I'll walk you back," Jaxson said.

Jaxson grabbed Iggy, and we headed to my apartment, via the ocean side this time. The warm sea breeze had cooled now that the sun had set, and it had left a trail of colors on the horizon. The view was stunning.

A while ago, we had planted a different hibiscus bush near the back entrance to the restaurant that appeared totally unscathed, which I found suspicious. I picked a few flowers that I hoped would help calm my iguana.

We walked upstairs and Jaxson motioned for Iggy to go inside.

"If you guys are going to kiss, I'm outta here."

I smiled and then turned to Jaxson. "He's not a romantic, is he?"

My boyfriend gathered me in his arms. "No, but I am."

Before I could respond, his lips were on mine, and I melted against him.

A moment later, he broke the kiss and moved away. "Tomorrow then?"

I smiled. "Yes."

Once inside, I gave Iggy the flowers. "I'm sorry you had a stressful day with Tippy."

"Every day is stressful."

"Speaking of stress, I'm going to take a bath and crawl into bed."

"I won't look."

What did that mean? Right now, nothing seemed to be making sense. "Night."

"Night." He munched on his flower, seemingly happy for now.

After I cleaned up and crawled into bed, I opened my e-reader to get caught up with my current book. I must have dozed off, because when I opened my eyes, a ghost was waving at me. I blinked a few times to make sure I wasn't imagining him. He looked familiar. "Wes Armstrong?"

"Finally, you're awake. You are a hard person to rouse. And it's not like I could tap you on the shoulder. Yes, it's me."

The realization that he'd come alone shocked my system into total alertness. I placed the e-reader on the nightstand.

"I'm sorry. Why are you here?"

"I dislike misinformation."

Now he had my entire attention. "Did you listen in to what I was saying—or rather hearing?" Can we say privacy issues?

He glanced to the side. "I do that only when necessary. I'm sorry. Honestly, I only snooped when you visited Harper Stiltman."

That was random. And why hadn't I seen him? "Why Harper?"

"He was married to my sister, and I was married to his sister."

If I'd been standing, I would have fallen over. "Come again?"

"Elaine Stiltman was my sister."

Never in a million years would I have guessed that. Irene might have been his enemy then. "I'm sorry for your loss." That sentiment just flew out of my mouth.

"Thank you. I know you think that I was putting the moves on your grandmother, but I was working for Harper to find out whether Adam was stealing from the company. I'm not some drunk or a womanizer. I'm a retired FBI agent—or rather I was. When Harper asked for my help, I agreed."

My mind was blown again. "Why Nana? She wouldn't have known a lot."

"Your grandmother was in touch with a lot of people. I didn't try to extract information only from her. I asked a lot of questions to Agnes as well."

"Does she know you were kind of a spy?"

I think he smiled. "She does now. Nothing gets past that

woman."

I had the sense he might have picked Pearl's brain, too, but I didn't want to ask. "Did you learn whether Adam had stolen the money?"

Mary had admitted that he had, and Harper seemed to agree, but I wanted to hear what he thought.

"He did." Wes flickered, disappearing for a few seconds before becoming visible again.

"Are you okay?"

He waved a hand, or rather what I guessed was his hand. "Yes. It's just that I'm only allowed so much time down here before I disappear completely."

"Really? Why?" I so wanted to learn about the afterlife, and this might be my only chance.

"Okay, since my time here is short, here's the thirty-second sound bite. If we aren't summoned in a séance, we can't leave until we have earned enough credits."

"What's a credit?" I only asked because it might be different than what it meant here.

"If you are nice to someone, show a lot of respect, or help others, you can earn credits. If say, you flirt too much—which is my downfall—then you lose credits."

Wow. "You all seem to come only at night. Is there a reason for that?"

"Yes. Only the ones with the most credits can show up during the day."

Maybe vampire ghosts did exist—only they weren't the biting kind. As much as I wanted to pick his brain forever, he flickered again. "Any suggestions where I should look to find Irene's killer?"

"We're working…on—" and then he disappeared.

"Wes?"

When he didn't reappear, I slumped against the head-board.

A few seconds later, Iggy came in. "The vampire ghosts are coming!"

Without an invitation, he crawled up on my bed. "What are you talking about?" I asked.

"I was awoken by a cold chill. I know that is the sign of a ghost."

Oh, my poor Iggy. "That was Wes."

"Wes? I didn't see him."

I wiggled my hand. "I'm wearing the ring, and you aren't."

He looked around. "There's no new world order happening in which the ghosts take over?"

I chuckled. "No, silly. Now go back to sleep, but wake me if you feel the cold again. Wes had a hard time rousing me, but you're good at it."

"I'm on it." Iggy jumped off my bed and waddled back to the living room.

I checked the clock. If it hadn't been two in the morning, I would have called Jaxson.

"You just woke up?" Rihanna asked the next day at the office. "Did you hear Wes call your name or feel the cold on your face?"

"I was in a dead sleep. I don't know what it was, but it

must have been something like that since I woke up." I told them all of the details I could remember, including the concept that ghosts needed credits to be able to come down to visit us.

"Good behavior gets them privileges?" Rihanna asked.

"Apparently."

Clearly, what happened in the afterlife was a bit more interesting to Rihanna than what else Wes had to say. "Back to my ghost sighting, Wes really seemed upset that there were lies being spread about him."

"He's no saint since he tried to worm his way into your grandmother's life, as well as a few other women's lives," Jaxson said. "It doesn't matter if he had a good reason."

"Yes, but he might have known that the stress was getting to his sister, and he wanted to save her."

"Or he was hoping that Irene would return to Adam if only to convince him to stop stealing. That way, Harper and Elaine could have their happily ever after," Rihanna offered.

I didn't buy her logic. People didn't act that way usually, but it wasn't my place to pass judgment on love. "All good thoughts. What I took away from this was that a ghost can watch what we're doing even if we can't see him." I looked around in case someone might be here now, but I sensed no cold chill." I turned to Iggy. "Let me know if you feel cold." Iggy was more sensitive to it that we were.

"I'm on it."

"What's our next step?" I asked. That seemed to be my all too common question of late.

"We might have to leave this case in the hands of the ghosts, especially if they are on it," Jaxson said.

"They might be searching for clues as we speak and only need us to meet face-to-face with people who are alive." I liked to think that when a witch or warlock passed over that they could still be involved with the comings and goings of this world.

"At this point, I'll believe anything," he said.

"Why hasn't Nana shown up?" Rihanna asked.

"I'd like to know the answer to that too."

Since we'd more or less exhausted all of our avenues, Jaxson and I spent the rest of the morning and part of the afternoon buying and then building a cage over the plants. It had to be removable so that we could pick the flowers and trim the bushes. Otherwise, the plant might just grow through the cage.

"I'm dirty and sweaty," I said once we were finished. "I'm going to shower and then come back." We had a shower here, but only Rihanna—and occasionally Jaxson—used it.

"Sure, see you in a few," he said.

I didn't bother asking Iggy if he wanted to come, since I wouldn't be gone long.

I'd just stepped out of the shower at my place and had wrapped a towel around me when I felt a cold chill cross my face. I stilled, but only for a moment when I realized it was still daylight. I figured it couldn't be a ghost—unless this one had a lot of credits.

Holding tight to my towel, I called out, "Hello?"

The small bathroom was filled with steam from my shower, so it was difficult to tell whether there really was a ghost here or not. I thought I might have better luck in the bedroom, so I reached out to open the door when my arm was suddenly encased in an icy block. Instantly, I retracted it. "Sorry."

"Open the door now," said a deep, disembodied voice.

This was a little creepy—okay, a lot creepy—but I did as he asked. I spotted my bathrobe on the bed, rushed over and grabbed it, and then slipped my hands in the sleeves. I didn't bother unknotting the towel. I spun around, but still saw no one.

"It's me, Neil Phillips." The voice wasn't coming from any one spot.

"Where are you?"

"I'm here, but not in any form you can see. That takes too many credits."

"Oh, okay. How can I help you?" Or was he here to help me?

"I'm certain that Adam Talbert was involved in his wife's death. He's not this weak person you all seem to think he is— before or after Irene was alive."

"Really? Then why did Irene leave him?" If Irene was up there with them, I would think they would have discussed it.

"Harper had more class than Adam, which Irene appreciated. Harper's family owned a large cattle ranch and was very wealthy."

Harper was now living at his family's estate. Interesting. "I've been there."

"Wes had told me a lot of tales about the ranch. According to Irene, Adam became jealous of Harper partly because of his wealth, and in part because of his ability to think on a bigger scale."

"But Adam was a talented marketer."

"Yes, but he didn't possess vision. That was what attracted Irene to Harper and Harper to her."

Too bad those two hadn't gotten together first instead of meeting their spouses, but I kept that thought to myself.

"You said you believe that Adam killed Irene?"

"I said I thought he was involved somehow. By that I mean, he knows who killed her. At least I'm pretty sure."

"Who do *you* think killed her?"

"If I knew that, I wouldn't be here. Until later."

"Wait!"

Why did ghosts disappear just when the conversation was getting good? I assumed he was gone, even though I couldn't see him. I waited for thirty seconds before grabbing my clothes and returning to the bathroom to change.

Not wanting to stay at my place any longer than necessary, I dressed and ran—or rather walked really fast—back to the office. Once I did the final sprint up the stairs, I was a sweaty mess again. As soon as I burst through the door, Jaxson shoved back his chair and rushed over to me. "What's wrong?"

"I saw a ghost." That almost cracked me up, though that hadn't been my intention. "Actually, I spoke to a ghost, but I didn't actually see him."

"Sit down and let me get you some tea."

Rihanna came out of her bedroom. "You look flushed."

"You would too if a ghost showed up in your bathroom. Thank goodness, I'd just wrapped a towel around me."

I sat on the sofa and looked around for my familiar. "Where's Iggy?"

Rihanna sat in her usual seat. "He's on border patrol."

Chapter Fifteen

"WHAT DOES ON *border patrol* mean?" I asked my cousin. Iggy believed he'd figured out when the seagulls were most likely to appear already.

"He's by the plants making sure that his *friends* don't mess with the hibiscus bushes you just planted."

"But we have a cage around the bushes."

Rihanna shrugged. Jaxson came out with my sweet tea and handed it to me. He then sat down next to me.

"Tell me about this ghost sighting. Did you know who it was?" Jaxson asked.

"He told me he was Neil Phillips, but I couldn't see him this time."

"Did he run out of credits?" Rihanna asked.

"I'm guessing, but I was more interested in learning what he had to say. I know these ghosts don't stay around for long."

I explained about Neil and his theory regarding Irene's death. "He seemed determined to point me in Adam's direction."

Jaxson whistled. "Are you thinking we should visit him again?"

"What would we ask him that we didn't ask him before? We know about Sally Gentran and now his partner's name, but I'm not sure Adam will say anything more than his wife keeps visiting him."

"Suggestions?"

"To quote Iggy: I got nothing."

Jaxson placed a hand on my arm. "How about we all get something to eat? You always think better on a full stomach."

I loved this man. He knew me so well. "Deal." I turned to my cousin. "You in?"

"You bet."

Once we reached the bottom of the steps, I looked for Iggy. It took some work, but I located him next to the cage. "Hey, how's it going?"

"It's working."

"What's working?"

"I haven't seen or heard a seagull since I've been down here."

I had planned to invite him to eat with us, but he wouldn't want to go to the rather upscale Magic Wand Hotel. "Keep up the good work."

"Aye, aye captain."

Where did he learn those sayings? Television, I guess. We walked across the street to the hotel. The service wasn't as fast as say the diner or the Tiki Hut Grill, but the food was excellent, and the peace would allow us to do some brainstorming.

We were seated in a corner booth, which would allow us to talk in relative privacy. Not only that, few others were there since it was a bit early for dinner. I checked out the menu, but after being approached by an invisible ghost, I found it hard to focus.

"Glinda?" Jaxson nodded to the waiter.

I looked up at the waiter looming over me. "Oh, sorry. I'll have a glass of Merlot."

"Of course."

The other two ordered. "Where did you go just now?" Jaxson asked once the waiter left.

"Just thinking about my encounter with Neil. It was a bit disturbing despite having seen and spoken with many ghosts before."

"Why was this time different?"

"I don't know. Maybe after a soothing glass of wine, I'll be relaxed enough to think of something."

The waiter returned promptly and placed the glass in front of me. After downing half of it, I was calm enough to look over the menu and order.

Halfway through my meal, I was feeling a lot better when out of nowhere a cold breeze kissed my face again. Without thinking, I grabbed Jaxson's and Rihanna's hands. "I feel something."

Both Jaxson and Rihanna looked around. In an instant, a woman appeared next to Rihanna. Where had she come from? Hold on. I knew her. "Jean Elkhart?" I don't know why I asked. I would have recognized her blue flowered dress anywhere.

"Yes, it's me, but I don't have much time. I have to get back soon."

"Back home?"

She smiled. "If you can call where my soul resides home, then yes."

What was she talking about?

With her free hand, Rihanna reached out to touch Jean, but when her arm went right through the woman, my heart rate spiked, and I almost hyperventilated.

"Are you a ghost?" I whispered.

"I am."

"How?" Jaxson asked. "You look solid. I mean, I just witnessed Rihanna put her hand through you, but you don't appear like any ghost we've ever seen."

She smiled. "I know. It took me a long time to earn enough credits to be able to do this, which is why I can't stay long. I am sorry for deceiving you."

"How did you deceive us?" Or was she talking about pretending to be real when she wasn't?

"My full name is Irene Jean Elkhart Talbert."

Shock almost caused me to let go of Jaxson's hand, but if I had, he wouldn't have been able to see her. "You're Irene? The Irene? The one who was mowed down on the road?"

I don't know why I kept asking the same question so many times.

"Yes."

"My grandmother is so worried about you."

"I know. I will go back shortly, I promise, but I am determined this time to find out who killed me. I have my suspicions, but I want proof. When Amelia told me how talented her two granddaughters were, I thought this was the perfect opportunity to find my killer."

My surprise at this statement knew no bounds. "Why not just tell us the truth?"

She grinned and winked. "It was more fun this way."

How had she earned so many credits if she thought like

that? I guess it didn't matter. She was here now. "What's the plan?"

"I want to confront Adam. I've learned a few things from what you've unearthed, and I've also been doing a lot of thinking."

That didn't sound like much of a plan. "What can we do?"

"I don't expect Adam to pay for anything he's done—whatever that is. We all can see his grip on reality is slipping, but I'm convinced he knows things. Mind you, I've gone to him several times. Sometimes he remembers me and sometimes he doesn't. I've been watching your two gargoyle friends, Hugo and Genevieve, and I think they can help."

"Watching them?" Rihanna asked. "What does that mean?"

"Let's say, I can psychically initiate a connection to them since they aren't fully human. It's a bit complicated. Ghost stuff and such."

Ghost stuff? If she didn't want to tell us, she wouldn't. "Do they know you've been connecting with them?" I thought that was an invasion of privacy if they didn't.

"Maybe, maybe not, but hear me out. I never make a connection lightly, but I'm desperate. I think this Genevieve gargoyle shifter can channel Adam's brain waves in such a way that he can remember what happened, if only for a short time."

I had no idea if she could do that or not. "Have you seen her do that?" If so, why hadn't Andorra mentioned it.

"No, but I can sense her potential. She has the ability to control electricity, and brain waves are basically electrical currents surging from one part of the brain to another."

That was really simplified, but I agreed with the gist of what she was saying. I just hoped Genevieve knew she could do something like that. "I can see how that might work."

Irene flashed me a smile. "Both she and Hugo have a lot of abilities. I'm hoping I can help teach them how to use their talents to do this for me."

"Are you like a ghost tutor?"

She chuckled. "Hardly, but I will be calling in all my favors from above to get this done. I won't be alone."

That was good to know.

"Suppose Genevieve agrees to help," Jaxson asked. "Then what?"

"I'll be able to find out what Adam knows. I just want to learn the truth. If he killed me, then so be it. No hard feelings."

Really? I'd be mad, but she might not be able to do anything about it, so why get riled up? I didn't know for sure if all ghosts needed closure, but maybe they did. "When would you like to do this brain controlling experiment?"

"Ideally, tomorrow, but I'll need to speak with Genevieve and Hugo first. These lessons may take a while."

That would be amazing to watch, but I doubt she'd let me observe. "What should we do in the meantime?"

"I don't think you need to do much."

That was disappointing.

"Would you mind if we put a recording device on Hugo or Genevieve when they give Adam's brain a memory boost so we can view what is happening in real time?" Jaxson asked.

"Be my guest. Do whatever you need to. I have a lot to

accomplish in a short time. I'll have Genevieve tell you the full plan tomorrow."

Before I could ask anything else, she disappeared. I let go of both of hands. When I glanced around the restaurant, no one seemed to have noticed anything. From an outsider's perspective, we were having a conversation with each other.

I drained my wine. "Is anyone's mind blown?"

"What do you think? You've had a year to adjust to seeing ghosts and other things, but I've experienced nothing like this, other than when I saw the four ghosts at your place, and again at the beach."

He had a point. "I hope it doesn't scar you for life."

He chuckled. "It's actually a good thing. I want to be part of your world, and this gives me the opportunity to do so."

"That's sweet. Thank you."

"I trust we'll be checking in with Genevieve and Hugo tomorrow to get the scoop?" Rihanna asked.

"That's what it seems like."

"We'll need to ask Steve for one of his recording devices so we can listen and maybe watch," Jaxson said. "It should be really interesting."

"I know that we can see Jean, or rather Irene, but do you think others can? She is still a ghost, only she took a more solid form."

"I guess we'll find out tomorrow," Jaxson said.

AT NINE THE next morning I was wide awake, something that hadn't happened in a while. The excitement of finding out who'd killed Irene had kept me from getting a good night's sleep. The best part of this sting operation was that I didn't have to do anything. Too often, the success or failure of a case depended heavily on some magic that I had to perform. In this case, our two gargoyles would be carrying the heavy load.

Fairly energized, I dressed. When I stepped into the living room, Iggy was asleep on his stool. "Wake up, sleepy head."

"Leave me alone."

I went over to him. "What's wrong?"

"I didn't get to sleep until late. Guarding the hibiscus plants took a lot out of me."

"Did Tippy or his friends show up at all?"

"No."

"Maybe you scared him off. I'm going to visit Hugo. You can stay here and get your beauty rest, or you can come with me. Which will it be?"

As if I'd doused him with ice water, his eyes popped open, and then he flew off his stool. "I'm ready."

I laughed. "We need to stop off at the office first. I want Rihanna and Jaxson to come with us."

"Okay, but why do we need to see Hugo?"

When I'd returned home last night, Iggy was already asleep. How much shuteye did a lizard really need? "We had a visitor at the restaurant last night."

"Who?"

"Irene." I bent down, lifted him up, and placed him in my bag.

"What did she say?"

I gave him the short version. "In theory, she is devising a plan in which Genevieve will tap into Adam's failing brain, and Hugo will help."

"That is so cool."

"I think so too."

When we reached the office, I checked to make certain the hibiscus plants were still intact. They were. If they hadn't been, my familiar would have gone ballistic.

Both Jaxson and Rihanna were up and about when I arrived. Jaxson nodded to the coffee on my desk. To my delight, steam was still pouring off the top. Was he now psychic? How did he know I was on my way, especially this early in the morning? I didn't dare ask. "You are the best."

"I am, aren't I?"

I blew on the top and took a small sip. Even that little bit of caffeine helped wake me up. "Give me a minute to ingest this, and then we can check to see what Genevieve and Hugo have planned."

"I already called Steve and asked for some equipment," Jaxson said. "When we go to00 the Hex and Bones, we'll have to stop at the sheriff's office to pick it up."

Chills ran through my body, and they weren't from any ghost. This was from excitement. I was always jazzed when a case was drawing to a close. I sat in my chair and sipped my coffee, trying to imagine how this would all work. "What happens if Genevieve, Hugo, and Irene are with Adam and the nurse shows up?" I asked.

"They'll be cloaked," Iggy said as he crawled out of my bag.

"I guess that's true. Then nothing can go wrong?"

"Assuming Hugo and Genevieve can draw the truth out of Adam, I only see a positive outcome," Jaxson said.

I didn't know why I was nervous then, but I was. I finished my coffee and placed the cup in the sink. When I returned, we left and headed across the street to the Hex and Bones where both Bertha and Andorra waved when we entered. I had to believe they found this as exciting as I did.

I didn't see Hugo or Genevieve, but I figured they were in the back planning their sting operation. I lifted Iggy out of my purse and let him find his friends.

"Did Genevieve tell you about Irene visiting us last night?" I asked both of them.

"She told us about it this morning," Andorra said.

"Are they really going to try to spark Adam's brain?" Bertha asked.

"That's the plan. Who knows if it will work?"

The door to the back room opened. "Want to join us?" Genevieve called out. "We need to do some planning."

I couldn't wait.

Chapter Sixteen

GENEVIEVE OR HUGO had already placed some chairs in a semi-circle, and Genevieve motioned we take a seat while both she and Hugo stood in front of the makeshift classroom.

She stood taller. "I'm sure Glinda told you about Irene visiting her, Jaxson, and Rihanna last night."

"Yes," Andorra and Bertha said in unison.

"Not me," Iggy piped up. "Glinda's mean. She's been leaving me out of everything."

"That is so not true. You were asleep last night when I came home. And I told you the short version on the way over. Listen carefully now."

He turned to face Hugo, who reached over and lifted him up. My heart sang. Those two were such good friends.

"Irene is in search of the truth about the night of her death, and she is certain Adam knows," Genevieve said. "Only he isn't totally of sound mind to be able to tell her. That's where Hugo and I come in."

I probably shouldn't interrupt her story, but I was really curious about her abilities. "Can you really stimulate the memory area of the brain?"

"I hope so. My specialty is electricity. To be honest, I

hope I don't fry his memory." She waited a beat and then laughed. "Only kidding. I will start off doing small pulses, trying to figure out the right area to prod."

"What will Hugo get to do?" Iggy sounded quite excited for his friend to be a star once more.

"Hugo has the most important role of all. Once Adam is thinking clearly, Hugo will do his magic and make—if that's even the right word—Adam tell the truth as he knows it."

"Then what?" I asked.

"Then we go home. Should I do more?" Genevieve seemed concerned that she hadn't understood her assignment.

I suppose if we learned who killed Irene, the case would be solved. "If you get the chance, can you find out about Sally Gentran, as well as how Harper's wife died? I know it was stated that she died of a heart attack, but I'm wondering if she had help." I wasn't sure how he'd know, but it wouldn't hurt to ask.

"I can try." Genevieve turned to Jaxson. "Irene said something about wearing some kind of recording device?"

"Yes. I'll pick it up from the sheriff after we finish here."

"To save you a trip, Hugo and I can go over there with you now."

She seemed to be in a hurry. "When is the big reveal going to happen?" I asked.

"As soon as we're wired up with the camera. Then Hugo and I will teleport to the nursing home."

"How will you let Irene know that you are ready to go?" I needed to know the details.

"We can't contact her, but she seems to have tapped into our minds. It's a bit unsettling, but she promised that once this was over, she would only contact us if it was majorly important."

I had no idea if gargoyle shifters cared about stuff like privacy, but I guessed they did. "You're good with all of this?"

"Of course. Hugo and I want to help."

"Thank you. Both of you," Andorra said. She looked over at us. "Shall we get these two hooked up?"

"Absolutely."

Bertha stayed behind to work the store. To avoid being seen just popping up in Steve's office, they walked over with us. While Iggy would have been perfectly fine with Hugo carrying him from the Hex and Bones to the sheriff's office, I thought it best if he rode in my purse. People often stopped and wanted to chat about Iggy and that would only delay us.

When we arrived, Steve must have told Pearl to expect us. "Steve is in the conference room with your equipment. This is going to be fantastic."

I smiled. "I hope we get answers."

"Me, too."

The seven of us went back to the conference room. We hadn't told Steve what to expect since we didn't know what was going to happen until Genevieve laid out her plan.

Steve welcomed us. "Have a seat and tell me how I can help, other than provide you with the equipment."

Genevieve briefly explained how she envisioned this operation going down. While Steve focused on her every word, I'm not sure he was believing all of it. Heck, even I was a bit skeptical.

"Let me see if I have this right. Adam Talbert's dead wife, Irene, will appear in a relatively human form in order to ask

Adam questions about her own death?"

"Yes," Genevieve said.

"You don't think Adam might go into shock when he sees his dead wife?" Steve asked.

I raised my hand. "He claims that Irene has shown up many times since her death—which she has. Often, he'll acknowledge that she's passed, and at other times, he doesn't recognize her."

Steve faced Genevieve again. "But that is where you come in, right?"

"Yes," she said. "I believe I can unscramble his brain for a short period of time. In the meantime, Hugo here will do his magic on Adam and get him to tell the truth."

"That sounds too easy," Steve said. "I've seen Hugo in action before, but will Adam remember anything afterward?"

"Our last suspect didn't, if you recall."

"I remember all right. You all know that we can't use any of this to prosecute the person Adam names?" We all nodded. "Okay, then let me hook you two up. I have two monitors set up to receive the recording. You said you will be invisible?"

"Yes," Genevieve said. "You won't see us since we'll be cloaked. In fact, if you can't see ghosts, you won't even see Irene. All you'll see is an old man talking to himself."

Steve shook his head and inhaled. "Let's do this." He put the small cameras on both Genevieve and Hugo. Since they would be invisible, he didn't bother trying to hide the equipment.

Genevieve turned to us. "Go ahead and turn on the cameras. We'll be rolling in a few seconds." With that they disappeared.

Steve huffed. "I will never get used to her doing that."

We laughed, probably because of the tension that had built around this whole case. Both cameras sprang to life. Adam was sitting in his chair with a blanket over his lap, and like before, he seemed to be asleep.

"Where's Irene?" I asked.

"She's probably waiting for the right moment to show up. I bet she doesn't want to interfere with what both Genevieve and Hugo need to do," Jaxson offered.

It was really strange to see one camera focused on the back wall and the other aimed at Adam's face. I had to assume that Genevieve was doing her magic on Adam while Hugo was standing by. After a few minutes, the cameras switched positions.

"Do you think it's Hugo's turn to get Adam to tell the truth?" I asked.

"I'm completely confused about what exactly is going to happen," Andorra admitted. "If this works, I'll be blown away."

When both cameras faced Adam, Irene magically appeared. "There she is." I sounded like a kid at Christmas.

Jaxson grabbed my hand. Shoot. I'd forgotten that unless we were connected, they wouldn't be able to see and hear anything. "Everyone hold hands. Steve, it's the only way to see Irene."

Without a word, he took Andorra's hand. "She's a ghost?" he asked. "She looks so alive."

I was thrilled that this worked. "I know. We were fooled by her too. If you try to touch her, your hand will go right through her. It's like she's a cloud."

"I'm not ready for that yet," he said.

Irene began to speak. "Adam, wake up."

After a few seconds of prompting, her husband opened his eyes. As soon as he saw her, he grabbed a hold of his chair. "Irene? What are you doing here? I mean, how are you here? You're dead!" He rubbed his eyes. "I must be dreaming."

Clearly, Genevieve's magic had worked. Let's hope Hugo was as successful.

"No, you aren't. I'm a ghost, but I took a human form to make it easier on you."

"What do you want?" The man sounded scared but mentally alert.

"I came in part to apologize."

Okay, I hadn't expected that.

"For what? For sleeping with my business partner?" His bitterness was evident.

"Yes. That was wrong of me. I should have told you I was unhappy with our marriage. I'm sorry."

He looked around, as if he thought he was in some kind of dream, despite Irene telling him otherwise. "Nothing can be done about it now."

"I know. Again, I'm sorry, but I need to know if you killed me, Adam?"

He jerked. "No. I loved you."

Her shoulders sagged. "Then who did? I know that you know."

He glanced to the side. "It was Sally."

I squeezed Jaxson's hand. I hadn't guessed it was her.

"Why did she do it? She didn't even know me."

He shook his head. "No, but she was positive that after

Harper told you he had to take care of Elaine, that you would waltz back into my life."

Her mouth slightly opened. "Didn't you tell her I had no intention of doing that?"

He shook his head. "I was too embarrassed to say that I couldn't keep you from leaving. I honestly thought that if I took enough money from the company that you'd stay."

"Seriously? After you stole from Harper?"

His head lowered. "I was desperate. I'm sorry."

Irene stepped forward, or rather she floated closer to him. "Did you know Sally was planning to kill me?"

He jerked upright. "No. Never."

"I guess I should be happy that she is in some place not as pleasant as where I am."

He nodded. "What she did was terrible, unspeakable, shameful, but don't worry. I'll be joining her soon."

"You? Why? You did nothing."

"Yes, I did," he said. "I killed Sally. Poisoned her, in fact," Adam said. "I couldn't let her get away with killing you."

What? Okay, I had not seen that coming either. I guessed Adam was stronger than he looked.

"I always thought you hated me for what I did. You should have been happy I was dead."

He reached out his hand, but Irene didn't move toward him to grab it. He must have realized that he couldn't touch a ghost, because he immediately lowered his arm.

"No, I always loved you, even if you loved Harper more."

Irene finally moved toward Adam, and then she seemed to disappear as soon as they touched. The cameras clicked off. "Really? It was just getting good," I blurted.

Steve fiddled with the monitor. "Either they turned them off, or…"

"Maybe they wanted to give Irene some privacy." Darn.

A second later, Genevieve and Hugo appeared. "Did you get it all?"

She actually sounded excited. I let go of Jaxson's hand since Irene was no longer around.

"Yes. Thank you." I wasn't sure what good it did, but I hoped that Irene had returned to witch Nirvana so that Nana could stop worrying.

Steve helped them take off their cameras. "If I replay this, will anything show up?" he asked.

"No, sir. This wasn't to put Adam in jail."

"I think he's been in his own jail for years," he said. "I can't imagine his pain of losing his wife, and then killing another person he cared about because she had killed his wife."

"What are you going to do now, Steve?" I asked.

"I plan to leave the case as unsolved. It isn't as if I can prove that any of this happened."

"True. I just hope this gives Irene the closure she was looking for," I said.

While it was early in the day, my body was bone weary from the stress. I pushed back my chair and stood. "Thank you all so much for helping my grandmother find her friend. I could use something to eat. Anyone want to join me?"

"Count me in," Jaxson said.

Andorra looked over at Hugo and seemed to be communicating with him. "Thanks for the invite, but the three of us will head back. I'm glad Irene's murder has finally been solved."

"Me, too."

We thanked Steve once more. Only then did I realize that this was the first time he'd seen a ghost and yet he appeared rather stoic. "Are you okay, Steve? My first ghost sighting rattled me for weeks."

"If you hadn't told me she was a ghost, I wouldn't have known. But when she disappeared, it was a bit disturbing. It will take a while to sink in."

"The world of the occult can be a strange place."

"You can say that again."

Once we headed out, I assumed Steve would fill Pearl in on the intriguing series of events. "Any suggestions where you'd like to eat?" I asked Jaxson and Rihanna.

"The Tiki Hut," Rihanna said. "Only Aunt Fern will be there to question us, and we can put her off until later if you wish."

As opposed to the other gossip queens, who would pester us until we cracked. "Don't forget Penny might be there, but I can fill her in later, too."

We grabbed a table in her section. "Are we missing anything? I feel as if something still needs to be done."

"I think Harper Stiltman would like some closure," Jaxson said.

"That's it. You're right."

Chapter Seventeen

AFTER WE FINISHED our meal, Jaxson and I headed out to Stiltman's ranch. I thought it best if Iggy stayed behind since we hadn't left on the best of terms. Rihanna also decided to stay back in town where it would be safe.

We were halfway to his ranch when I twisted in my seat toward Jaxson. "How do you think he'll react when we tell him that Sally killed Irene?"

"I don't think he'll show any emotion. Both women he loved are gone. Knowing who killed Irene might help, or it might not. I think I'm doing this more to dot all our I's and cross our T's."

"That works for me. You know how much I dislike loose ends."

Jaxson reached over and clasped my hand. "I do."

This time when we pulled into the drive, we found Harper Stiltman sitting on his porch—with a woman, no less. Dare I believe he decided to come out of his self-imposed asylum for a while? He wouldn't be aware that we'd learned who'd killed Irene yet.

Jaxson parked.

"Mr. Stiltman?" Jaxson called as we approached. "May we have a word?"

"Of course." He actually sounded happy—or at least not as mad as he was when we last saw him.

We stepped onto to the porch. "We came to tell you about who killed Irene."

His eyes widened. "You found out? Who was it?"

Jaxson looked over at the woman who appeared to be younger than him.

"Oh, you can say anything in front of Janie. She's my sister and was Wes Armstrong's wife."

I turned to her. "I'm sorry for your loss."

"Did you know Wes?"

Since we'd already told Harper about seeing ghosts, he probably had shared the information with her. "Only in his ghost form. He seemed happy."

She sagged against her seat. "I am so glad. Did he help find out what happened to Irene?"

"He did." In an indirect way.

Harper motioned we take a seat. We then proceeded to tell him about Adam's confession. "He admitted to poisoning Sally because she'd run over Irene. And Sally killed Irene because she was jealous."

"Sally had nothing to be jealous about. Irene had no intention of remaining with Adam."

"Adam was too embarrassed to tell Sally that."

Jaxson leaned forward. "Just so you know, Adam confessed to stealing company funds, too. He didn't claim it had anything to do with not wanting the company to expand, but I'm guessing it was to entice Irene to want to be with him."

Harper dragged a hand down his jaw. "Adam was in denial most of his life. My biggest regret was in partnering with him in the first place." He coughed. "Excuse me. I thought Adam's mind had deteriorated."

I didn't think explaining about gargoyles was appropriate. "We caught him on a good day."

Harper nodded. "Thank you for letting me know."

When he let out a breath and sagged against the chair, I felt that was our cue to leave. Without saying anything more, we headed out.

As soon as I climbed in the front seat, Jaxson fired up the engine and drove back to town. "That went kind of well, don't you think?" I asked.

"As well as can be expected. I hope he can rest easier now. I also hope his sister can encourage him to get out of the house more often."

"I hope so, too. I'm glad she reached out." He could have called her, but somehow I doubted that.

Once back in town, Jaxson said he wanted to stop off at the office. "Maybe afterward we can relax at your place and watch a movie."

"I'd like that." It would make a great afternoon.

As soon as we stepped inside the office, we found Iggy pacing. He stopped. "How did it go?" he asked.

Just as I started to fill him in on Mr. Stiltman's reaction, my necklace pulsed. I clasped the pink gem and looked around. "Nana?"

Jaxson came over, and I clasped his hand with my ring hand. If my grandmother appeared, he'd be able to see her.

"Is she here?" he asked. "I'd love to meet her."

Iggy scurried up my leg and then up my arm to reach my shoulder.

Nana's image wavered. "Oh, Glinda. I can't thank you enough for helping Irene. Her death has been a cloud over her head for so long."

"She's back then?" Of course she was. If she hadn't returned, Nana probably wouldn't know that the case had been solved.

"Yes. She wanted me to thank you again."

"We were happy to help."

Jaxson squeezed my hand. "Hi, I'm Jaxson, Glinda's partner."

Nana smiled. "I know who you are, young man, and I couldn't be happier you two are together. It's what makes my being gone easier."

A hand touched my shoulder, and I almost jumped.

"Nana?" Rihanna asked.

"Rihanna, darling. There you are. You are so like your father. I couldn't be prouder of you. Even if I used all of the credits I've accumulated over the years, I still couldn't hug you, and that is one of my biggest wishes."

"I wish that, too, Nana."

"Glinda, you should know that the ring you are wearing was given special powers right before my friends descended on you at the party. It had no power before your birthday, and once I leave, it will once more be powerless."

Disappointment washed over me. "I thought I could contact you with this ring."

"I'm sorry, my sweet child." She flickered a bit. "I must be going. I'll have to work on doing more good deeds so I can return and chat." With that she left.

We released our hold on each other. While I had spoken

to my grandmother many times in the last year, this time seemed different. I turned to Rihanna. "How did she seem to you?"

"Seem? Melancholy but happy."

Those two words were opposites to me. "Perhaps more like resigned that she couldn't be with us, but happy that we'd done well for ourselves." I grabbed Jaxson's hand and squeezed.

"Tell me how the discussion with Mr. Stiltman went," Rihanna asked.

We gave her the rundown. "I think he finally has closure. I'm hoping with the help of his sister, he can move on."

"I hope so. Gavin is going to call me in a few minutes, so I need to go, but I'll see you tomorrow?"

We didn't have a case, but we both usually showed up to work anyway. Who knew what new event would fall into our laps? "Absolutely."

Just as she returned to her bedroom, a loud squawking noise sounded outside our door. Iggy spun toward the entrance and froze.

"It's Tippy," he said with disgust.

"He can't hurt you if you are inside."

Iggy lifted his chest. "I'm not going to hide anymore."

A tap sounded on the cat door, followed by what sounded like a battle cry. Oh, my.

Iggy spun around. "I'm done with him."

"What are you going to do?"

"This." Iggy flew out the cat door.

My heart raced. Iggy was no match for one seagull, let alone if more than one showed up. The screeching subsided a few seconds later, and I had to assume that Tippy had flown away.

My familiar popped back in through the cat door. "That's it. He's pushed me too far."

I didn't see any evidence of damage on Iggy's face or body. "What are you planning to do?"

"I'm going to start a petition to ban all seagulls from the beach."

I had to swallow a laugh. "I don't think even the mayor has the power to order that. Seagulls never listen."

"You got that right, but I'm going to try anyway."

Since Iggy couldn't write, I wasn't sure how he was going to accomplish this. "Go for it."

With that encouragement, he shot out the door again, and I mentally wished him luck.

Jaxson turned me to face him. "Speaking of going for it, what do you say about us trying to go for it all?"

My knees nearly buckled, but with my luck, he was only talking about going to some fancy restaurant and ordering the entire menu. "What exactly does that entail?"

He grinned. "You know how much I love you, right?"

He didn't say it often, but when he did, he meant it. "Yes, and I love you too."

"Good." He pulled a small box out of his pocket, and when he dropped to one knee, I had to lock my legs to keep from falling.

He opened the box to expose a gorgeous diamond ring, and I couldn't help but suck in a breath. "It's beautiful."

"Not half as beautiful as you. It was my grandmother's."

"Wow." Shock had a way of tongue-tying me.

"Glinda Goodall, will you do the honor of being my wife?"

All I could do was squeal. When he dipped his chin, I guess he wanted an answer. "Yes, yes, and yes."

Jaxson laughed, stood, and then lifted me up and spun me around. "You just made me the happiest man in the world."

"And you made me the happiest woman."

The kiss that followed confirmed it.

What's next? Someone steals a very valuable pink pearl necklace from a rich heiress. A few days later, during a scuba diving adventure, she doesn't surface. Since the necklace has magical powers, Glinda and her team are called in to help.

Buy on Amazon or read for FREE on Kindle Unlimited

Don't forget to sign up for my Cozy Mystery newsletter *to learn about my discounts and upcoming releases. If you prefer to only receive notices regarding my releases, follow me on BookBub.*
http://smarturl.it/VellaDayNL
bookbub.com/authors/vella-day

Here is a sneak peek of book 15: Pilfering the Pink Pearls

"I WANT TO report a crime. Someone *stole* my pink pearl necklace, which was *locked* in my hotel room's safe." The woman's voice grew louder with each word.

That irate guest was in the lobby of the Magic Wand Hotel, and her voice was close to a shout. Since the front desk was just out of sight of the hotel restaurant where Jaxson Harrison and I were having dinner to celebrate our one month engagement, we could hear her quite clearly. Naturally, I wanted to see who was making this allegation, but that would be rude. Why? Because I wanted this dinner to be about us—not our job.

In case you're wondering why I would care, I'm Glinda

Goodall, half owner of the Pink Iguana Sleuths agency. Whenever I hear of a potential crime, my ears perk up.

I turned to my business partner and fiancé. "I can't remember hearing about any thefts in this hotel before. Have you?"

"No. Ted and Nate run a tight ship. You planning to find out what's going on?" His cute little smirk implied he knew I wanted to.

"No. This is our time." I held up my glass of wine and tapped it against his beer bottle, proud that I wanted to put our date above my curiosity.

"I greatly appreciate the gesture, but I have the sense I won't have your full attention until you get a visual on this woman. Go ahead. When you return, you can tell me all about it." Jaxson leaned back in his chair and held up his beer.

I could argue, but he'd insist—or at least I hope he would. "You know me too well."

He grinned. "I do. Now go."

I almost giggled, which probably wasn't all that classy for a twenty-eight-year old. Regardless, I pushed back my chair and headed out to the lobby. I wanted to look like I was a guest and not like someone interested in the drama unfolding at the reception desk. Too bad I was never great at the cloak and dagger stuff.

All I needed was a peek, so I shot a quick glance in her direction. A moderately good-looking gentleman and a tall, attractive woman were standing at the front desk. The man didn't appear all that interested in what the lady was saying since he was studying the rack of keys behind the clerk instead of paying attention to the complaint.

The female guest was a different matter. She was leaning over the desk, her palms planted on the surface. Her dark hair was pulled back in a ponytail, and except for the large, teardrop diamond earrings, I might have thought she was about to go for a run. The tight black pants were topped with a fitted, light blue sleeveless shirt that looked like something one would see on the cover of a fitness magazine—not that I looked at many of those. Working out wasn't my thing.

The forty-something-year old woman had both muscles and beauty and appeared to be the one in charge since the man wasn't saying anything. The man, on the other hand, was dressed in a pair of dark charcoal gray pants and a white button-down shirt. I'd put him a good fifteen years older than the woman.

"What are you going to do about this travesty?" The owner of the necklace asked, clearly incensed. She didn't seem to have a problem taking out her anger on the poor employee either.

I wasn't impressed with her rather rude—or maybe I should say desperate—approach, but if the necklace was as valuable as she made it out to be, I might be upset too. If someone took my grandmother's magical pink pendant, I'd be a total basket case, and I might even be raising my voice. A lot.

The man looked up and lasered me with a stare. Whoops. Caught. Having no desire for him to come over and question me, I walked over to one of the side tables next to the hotel's seating area, picked up a random fishing magazine, and flipped through the pages, pretending as if I was totally fascinated with it. I hoped he believed I was just a guest wanting to know the ins and outs of tarpon fishing.

The man must have told the woman she was making a scene because she lowered her voice, and my ability to snoop dropped close to zero.

While Jaxson and I didn't eat here often, the same two or three clerks always worked the reception desk. Unfortunately, tonight, a new employee was there, which made extracting any gossip less than certain. I felt sorry for the young girl, but she seemed to be handling it as well as could be expected.

After a proper amount of time, I turned around and returned to the restaurant, making sure not to glance their way.

"Well?" Jaxson asked as soon as I sat down.

I told him my impression of the woman. "I just hope they can find the thief."

"What are you going to do about it?"

That brought a smile to my lips. "Who says I'm going to do anything?"

"Glinda Goodall. You wouldn't be you if you didn't want to know what happened and then try to help."

"True, but this seems to be something for our sheriff's department to handle."

"Uh-huh."

"Fine. I'll ask our gossip queens tomorrow what they know, but for tonight, I want this dinner to be about us."

Jaxson tilted his head. "What's going on? Your romantic side is showing." He smiled. "I have to say, I like it."

"Funny man." I wanted to change the subject—or rather needed to. "On a different note, I'm worried about Iggy."

Iggy is my familiar who is a pink iguana—and yes, I am a

witch. I still suffer some guilt over the fact that my spell turned him from green to pink. To this day, Iggy is a bit sensitive about his color, not that I can blame him. At least my familiar can talk and do a lot of other things that no ordinary iguana can.

Jaxson sat up straighter. "Why are you worried? He seems fine to me, other than he's on constant alert for his nemesis, Tippy."

Tippy was this rather distinctive seagull with black-tipped wings who seemed determined to harass my familiar—or so Iggy claimed. "For the last two weeks, he's been sleeping under the hibiscus tree by the office to make sure the seagulls don't eat the flowers."

"But he's sleeping, right?"

"I guess. It's warm this time of year, but what happens when winter comes?" Florida has been known to have a freeze or two. That kind of weather would kill Iggy.

"I'll talk with him. How is his petition to ban all seagulls from the beach coming?" Jaxson swallowed a smile.

We both knew that was a joke, but we all humored Iggy. Ever since the seagull leader—Tippy—pooped on him a time or two, my poor sixteen-year-old iguana couldn't focus on anything but getting his revenge. That was a tall mountain to climb since Iggy couldn't fly.

When my cousin, Rihanna, my Aunt Fern, and our witch friend Andorra helped collect signatures to present to the mayor, everyone thought it was cute. And yes, they recognized it for what it was—something to appease the agitated iguana.

"The mayor will put Iggy off for as long as he can, but at some point Iggy will catch on that nothing can be done about his problem," I said.

The most bizarre thing about this petition was that the mayor didn't really believe Iggy could talk. Why? Because only witches, warlocks, and some other special people could communicate with him. And the mayor was only a human.

"I bet if we offer our services to this woman to help find her necklace, Iggy will want to be involved. He's always more energized when we have a case."

Jaxson had a point. "True, but let's see what the sheriff comes up with first." We often ended up being involved in Steve Rocker's cases anyway, especially if there was an element of magic. "If we knew the occult was somehow a part of this, I'd offer our assistance right away."

"Sounds like a plan."

Not really, but I was determined not to dwell on it any more tonight. I wanted to celebrate being with Jaxson.

I waited until after we finished our meal before I suggested we speak with the desk clerk to get the scoop on this woman's complaint. Unfortunately, the shift had changed. Darn. Tomorrow, I was determined to find out more.

THE NEXT MORNING, I awoke to bright light streaming in through my bedroom window, which meant I'd overslept. I usually sleep in late, but this was late even for me. I realized we didn't have a case, but since my nineteen-year-old cousin, Rihanna, was attending classes at the nearby community college, Jaxson would be at the office by himself—assuming he decided to go into work today. If we were without a case, he often would wander downstairs to his brother's wine and cheese shop to help out.

I whipped off my covers, dressed, and got ready to face the day. "Iggy?" I called out as I went into the living room.

No answer. I looked around but didn't see him. I then checked the kitchen. My one-bedroom apartment only had three rooms—or more like two and a half since the kitchen was kind of an extension of the living room. Where was my familiar?

Considering it was later than usual, he either was visiting his girlfriend, Aimee, who was the talking cat that lived with my Aunt Fern across the hallway, or he'd already waddled over to the office. As much as he would have liked to be at the Hex and Bones Apothecary visiting Hugo, one of our resident gargoyle shifters, Iggy knew that crossing a busy street was dangerous. Being less than three-inches tall, it was difficult to see him even though he was pink.

Since my iguana could take care of himself for the most part, I walked to the office, which was a mere two buildings away. When I arrived, Jaxson was at his computer. Good.

I leaned over and kissed his cheek. "Good morning, or should I say good afternoon?"

He swiveled around in his chair and grinned. "You slept well, I take it?"

"I did. I'm sorry I'm late, but I kind of conked out after our wonderful dinner date last night."

He smiled. "I did, too."

As much as I wanted to rehash the part of the evening that had been romantic, I still wasn't comfortable with talking about intense emotions despite being engaged to him.

I refocused on something less personal. On his computer screen sat a weather map. "What are you working on?"

"I heard about a hurricane forming in the Atlantic."

I hissed in a breath and leaned closer. Hurricanes were always scary for Floridians. Thankfully, since we lived on the west side of Florida, we didn't get as many as the east coast did. "That's not good."

"No, and while we haven't had a direct hit in my lifetime, we can get high winds that can do a lot of damage."

"I know. When is the next one expected to arrive?"

"She's called tropical storm Irma, and she might not even come up the Gulf. If she does though, she won't be here for another two days."

"Good. We need to make sure that Aunt Fern has the boards ready to batten down the hatches if the storm heads this way."

He nodded. "I'll help."

"That would be great."

Jaxson looked around. "Where's Iggy? He didn't come with you?"

"No. He wasn't at the apartment when I got up either. I thought he might be here. Since he's not, he's probably visiting Aimee. I should have checked, but I hadn't had my morning coffee or any breakfast—or should I say, lunch—yet."

He leaned back and smiled. "Would you like to grab some food now?"

"I do like a man who can read my mind. How about the diner?" I was certain Iggy would be fine. He might even be out and about looking for Tippy.

"You got it. I'm assuming you plan to find out if Dolly knows anything about the pearl necklace heist at the hotel last night?"

"Of course, I am. I figure by now, Steve will have already investigated, which means information should have already spread by now." The gossip queen chain was very strong in Witch's Cove.

We were amateur sleuths after all, and as such, we were experts at knowing the right people to talk with. Dolly Andrews, the owner of the Spellbound Diner, was one such person, and she was always willing to impart and receive gossip. Since she was good friends with Pearl Dillsmith, the sheriff's grandmother and receptionist, we received a lot of good info from her.

Jaxson pushed back his chair. "I have to say I'm surprised Iggy isn't here. You did tell him about the heist last night, didn't you?"

"No, he was asleep when I got home."

"I'm sure he's heard about it by now, which means he'll be back to get the details."

"I imagine he will," I said.

I thought about leaving a note telling him where we would be—and yes he can read—but I didn't need him prancing into the diner. Despite wearing a collar, visitors might freak if they spotted a lizard in an eating establishment.

Jaxson and I headed down the stairs. At the bottom, I scanned all of the freshly planted hibiscus bushes to see if any animals had attacked the plants—plants that served as Iggy's favorite food. What I didn't expect was to see my familiar asleep under one of the bushes. I tapped Jaxson's shoulder.

He nodded. "I should have known."

"Me, too. He probably got up early and came over here to finish his nap, thinking his mere presence would deter the seagulls. For all I know, it does. Let's leave him be." We remained quiet as we headed to the diner, which was a short walk down the main street.

Every time I stepped into Dolly's old-fashioned establishment, it took me back to my childhood where I would sit at the counter with my parents or grandmother, drinking a chocolate shake. I remember Dolly always had a smile on her face. Her father had started the diner, and she'd picked up where he left off.

When we entered, I waved to her, and she came around the counter to greet us, like she did most of her guests.

"Hey, you guys. Let me see it," Dolly said.

I had no idea what she was talking about. "See what?"

She rolled her eyes. "Your engagement ring."

I couldn't believe I hadn't shown it to her before. I'd had the ring a month, but part of the time, the ring had been at the jewelers being sized. "Oh, this old thing?" I chuckled. "It was Jaxson's grandmother's ring. Isn't it gorgeous?" I wiggled the fingers on my ring hand.

"Totally. I couldn't be happier for you guys."

"Thanks, Dolly."

"Have a seat anywhere, and I'll be over to take your order."

I was hoping she would do more than just provide us with food. Gossip was my game today.

We sat in our usual booth. "I'm surprised she didn't mention the theft. Surely, Pearl would have told her about it."

Nothing got by Pearl—or almost nothing.

"Maybe she thinks we already know what happened at the hotel last night and plans to pick our brains," he said.

"It wouldn't be the first time, and yes, I know, gossip is a two-way street."

A few minutes later Dolly returned. "Sorry about that. I bet you've heard about that poor woman at the Magic Wand Hotel who had her necklace stolen last night."

I nodded. "We have, but I don't know much. Do you have the scoop?"

"Not really. Pearl said that the woman who was robbed was some rich heiress from Atlanta who runs a vitamin company. I think Pearl did a little research and found the woman was some distant relative to the Coca Cola fortune."

No wonder she was rich—assuming she inherited any family money. I had to chuckle. "And here you didn't think you knew much."

She smiled. "I meant, I wish I knew more."

I looked over at Jaxson. "It's more than I know. My only contribution is that I saw her at the front desk when she told the clerk that someone had taken her pearl necklace from her locked safe."

Dolly acted as if she'd learned that too. "She's supposed to be some fitness guru. Is she stunning?"

"Totally. She is tall, thin, and fit. And yes, beautiful."

Dolly sighed. "It's unfair for one person to be rich and good looking."

I glanced over at Jaxson and sighed. "I'm rich since I have a wonderful man in my life." I reached out and clasped his hand.

"That's twice in a twenty-four hour period that you've been romantic," he said.

He was right about that. Jaxson was usually the one to talk more about love than I was. "You bring it out in me."

"Okay, you two." Dolly sounded a little embarrassed. "Promise you'll let me know if you learn anything?"

"Of course. Pearl didn't tell you anything else?"

She tapped her pencil on her pad. "Not much other than Steve and Nash are on the case. It is a theft, so they have to investigate."

"If someone stole this woman's necklace from the hotel safe, it could be long gone by now."

Dolly nodded. "Sad but true."

By the time we finished ordering, I'd made up my mind. I wanted to help this lady find what was rightfully hers.

BUY Pilfering the Pink Pearls on AMAZON

THE END

A WITCH'S COVE MYSTERY (Paranormal Cozy Mystery)

PINK Is The New Black (book 1)

A PINK Potion Gone Wrong (book 2)

The Mystery of the PINK Aura (book 3)

Box Set (books 1-3)

Sleuthing In The PINK (book 4)

Not in The PINK (book 5)

Gone in the PINK of an Eye (book 6)

Box Set (books 4-6)

The PINK Pumpkin Party (book 7)

Mistletoe with a PINK Bow (book 8)

The Magical PINK Pendant (book 9)

The Poisoned PINK Punch (book 10)

PINK Smoke and Mirrors (book 11)

Broomsticks and PINK Gumdrops (book 12)

Knotted Up In PINK Yarn (book 13)

Ghosts and PINK Candles (book 14)

Pilfered PINK Pearls (book 15)

The Case of the Stolen PINK Tombstone (book 16)

The PINK Christmas Cookie Caper (book 17)

SILVER LAKE SERIES (3 OF THEM)

(1). HIDDEN REALMS OF SILVER LAKE (Paranormal

Romance)

Awakened By Flames (book 1)

Seduced By Flames (book 2)

Kissed By Flames (book 3)

Destiny In Flames (book 4)

Box Set (books 1-4)

Passionate Flames (book 5)

Ignited By Flames (book 6)
Touched By Flames (book 7)
Box Set (books 5-7)
Bound By Flames (book 8)
Fueled By Flames (book 9)
Scorched By Flames (book 10)

(2). **FOUR SISTERS OF FATE: HIDDEN REALMS OF SILVER LAKE** (Paranormal Romance)
Poppy (book 1)
Primrose (book 2)
Acacia (book 3)
Magnolia (book 4)
Box Set (books 1-4)
Jace (book 5)
Tanner (book 6)

(3). **WERES AND WITCHES OF SILVER LAKE**
(Paranormal Romance)
A Magical Shift (book 1)
Catching Her Bear (book 2)
Surge of Magic (book 3)
The Bear's Forbidden Wolf (book 4)
Her Reluctant Bear (book 5)
Freeing His Tiger (book 6)
Protecting His Wolf (book 7)
Waking His Bear (book 8)
Melting Her Wolf's Heart (book 9)
Her Wolf's Guarded Heart (book 10)
His Rogue Bear (book 11)
Box Set (books 1-4)

Box Set (books 5-8)
Reawakening Their Bears (book 12)

OTHER PARANORMAL SERIES
PACK WARS (Paranormal Romance)
Training Their Mate (book 1)
Claiming Their Mate (book 2)
Rescuing Their Virgin Mate (book 3)
Box Set (books 1-3)
Loving Their Vixen Mate (book 4)
Fighting For Their Mate (book 5)
Enticing Their Mate (book 6)
Box Set (books 1-4)
Complete Box Set (books 1-6)

HIDDEN HILLS SHIFTERS (Paranormal Romance)
An Unexpected Diversion (book 1)
Bare Instincts (book 2)
Shifting Destinies (book 3)
Embracing Fate (book 4)
Promises Unbroken (book 5)
Bare 'N Dirty (book 6)
Hidden Hills Shifters Complete Box Set (books 1-6)

CONTEMPORARY SERIES
MONTANA PROMISES (Full length contemporary
Romance)
Promises of Mercy (book 1)
Foundations For Three (book 2)
Montana Fire (book 3)
Montana Promises Box Set (books 1-3)

Hart To Hart (Book 4)
Burning Seduction (Book 5)
Montana Promises Complete Box Set (books 1-5)

ROCK HARD, MONTANA (contemporary romance novellas)
Montana Desire (book 1)
Awakening Passions (book 2)

PLEDGED TO PROTECT (contemporary romantic suspense)
From Panic To Passion (book 1)
From Danger To Desire (book 2)
From Terror To Temptation (book 3)
Pledged To Protect Box Set (books 1-3)

BURIED SERIES (contemporary romantic suspense)
Buried Alive (book 1)
Buried Secrets (book 2)
Buried Deep (book 3)
The Buried Series Complete Box Set (books 1-3)

A NASH MYSTERY (Contemporary Romance)
Sidearms and Silk(book 1)
Black Ops and Lingerie(book 2)
A Nash Mystery Box Set (books 1-2)

STARTER SETS (Romance)
Contemporary
Paranormal

Author Bio

Love it HOT and STEAMY? Sign up for my newsletter and receive MONTANA DESIRE for FREE. smarturl.it/o4cz93?IQid=MLite

OR Are you a fan of quirky PARANORMAL COZY MYSTERIES? Sign up for this newsletter. smarturl.it/CozyNL

Not only do I love to read, write, and dream, I'm an extrovert. I enjoy being around people and am always trying to understand what makes them tick. Not only must my romance books have a happily ever after, I need characters I can relate to. My men are wonderful, dynamic, smart, strong, and the best lovers in the world (of course).

My Paranormal Cozy Mysteries are where I let my imagination run wild with witches and a talking pink iguana who believes he's a real sleuth.

I believe I am the luckiest woman. I do what I love and I have a wonderful, supportive husband, who happens to be hot!

Fun facts about me

(1) I'm a math nerd who loves spreadsheets. Give me numbers and I'll find a pattern.

(2) I live on a Costa Rica beach!

(3) I also like to exercise. Yes, I know I'm odd.

I love hearing from readers either on FB or via email (hint, hint).

Social Media Sites

Website: www.velladay.com
FB: facebook.com/vella.day.90
Twitter: @velladay4
Gmail: velladayauthor@gmail.com